BOATS, BODIES AND THE BEES KNEES

BOATS, BODIES AND THE BEES KNEES

JANE GORMAN

EBook ISBN 978-0-9991100-5-8

Paperback ISBN 978-0-9991100-6-5

For my brother

❧ 1 ❧

"The police found a body on the banks of Spicer Creek." Anna McGregor couldn't help but shudder as she read aloud. "Not another death..." Her voice trailed off as she skimmed the few details provided in the news report. "Died yesterday evening... could be a drowning. Police are calling it a suspicious death... victim identified as Oliver Humphreys-Gibbons. Wow." She looked up from the newspaper and forced a smile. "That's quite a name, isn't it?" Her efforts to act untroubled by the news were for nothing. She was talking to herself. "Luke?"

"Meow."

She looked down to see she wasn't alone after all. Tough Cookie looked up at her and blinked.

"It's not a big deal, is it? Nothing to worry about, right?"

When the cat didn't respond, she decided to try the question out on Luke instead. Folding the paper to keep the article front and center, she hopped off the tall stool and went in search of her handyman. The lounge and dining room were empty but for a used coffee cup one of her guests must have set on the sideboard as they left her bed-and-breakfast that morning. She grabbed the cup and placed it in the sink on her way back through the kitchen to the mudroom off the side of the house.

"Luke," she said to the man who stood at the deep utility sink, scrubbing something. "Did you hear about this?"

"About what?"

Luke Arnold turned to her, and she felt the usual flutter.

He put one hand on the edge of the sink as he straightened, a sly grin cutting across his face, his green eyes bright above his lightly stubbled, chiseled jaw. As he moved, his muscles tensed under his white T-shirt and worn jeans. Anna couldn't help but notice that one of his back pockets was torn and hanging loose.

Her cousin, Eoin, stood on a step stool next to him, giving the eight-year-old just enough height to put his arms in the sink. He wore one of the short-sleeve button-down shirts he favored, and the edges of his sleeves and front of his shirt were soaked through. Anna wondered if whatever he was washing could be as wet as he was. The young Irish boy was a whiz at producing bizarre facts he picked up through his extensive reading or by listening to people talk around him—facts he kept neatly recorded in a worn notebook that Anna could see sticking out of his pocket at that moment—but he was not the best at manual labor.

"They found a body," Anna repeated. "On the banks of Spicer Creek."

"Are you serious?" Luke's eyes widened. "Another death in Cape May? That's not normal."

The historic New Jersey beach town that drew visitors

from around the world was known for its Victorian mansions, picturesque main street, and wide beaches, not mysterious deaths—at least not until then.

"I know. Should we be worried about Cape May's reputation? The body was found on the banks of the creek, caught on a branch. It must have been floating in the water and..." She shook her head and forced a smile. "At least all of my guests are safe and accounted for."

She didn't want to pretend the man's death didn't matter, but she didn't want to scare Eoin either. Plus, she didn't know how much more tragedy she could take. Her very first guest at the B and B had died at her breakfast table, and while that case had been solved—with no small amount of help from her and her friends—she didn't know if she had the mental and emotional strength to handle another murder so soon.

Luke grabbed a towel and dried his work-roughened hands as he came toward her, leaning close to read the article over her shoulder. He smelled of sawdust, sweat, and something sweet Anna couldn't place. She took another breath, a deep one, then returned her attention to the horrible news.

"Do they say who it was?" Luke asked.

"Yes, here. It's quite a name. The police have identified the victim as Oliver Humphreys-Gibbons, a guest at Congress Hall. You've been doing some work for them, haven't you?" Anna turned toward Luke. She knew he'd been hired by the popular local hotel to do some minor repairs around the building. "How's that going?"

Luke didn't respond, his eyes focused on the article, a deep frown etched onto his face.

"Are you okay?" Anna asked.

He straightened with a start, shook his head as if

ridding himself of a thought, and walked back to the sink. He dropped the towel on the edge of the basin and laughed. "Sure, yeah. What else does the article say about the man?"

Anna knew Luke well enough to recognize his laugh was forced, his eyes worried. She turned her attention back to the news. "Well, he checked into the hotel on Wednesday. He's in his forties. Um... not much else, actually."

Luke stood at the sink, staring intently at the blank wall in front of him. Eoin, rubbing his hands on the front of his shorts to dry them, looked up at the handyman.

"Why? What's going on?" Anna asked.

"Oliver Humphreys-Gibbons," Luke said as if talking to himself. "Was that it?"

"Was what it?" Anna put her hands on her hips, crumpling the newspaper in her fist. "Talk to me, Luke." Even as she said it, she realized she sounded unreasonable. Luke was her handyman, her friend, but nothing more. He didn't owe her an explanation. "At least tell me if you're okay, if I can do anything to help."

Luke turned to look at her, and Anna was relieved to see the familiar sly grin. Unfortunately, it didn't last.

He frowned as he walked past her into the kitchen. "I'm fine." He patted her on the shoulder as he passed. "I just need to get back to work. That's all."

Anna threw her hands in the air in frustration. She may not have known Luke long—she'd only moved to Cape May in January—but they'd spent enough time together for her to know he was lying.

She trotted after him into the kitchen and almost tripped over Tough Cookie as the cat weaved figure eights around her bowl sitting next to the lounge door. She meowed again, loudly, and put a firm paw on Anna's leg.

Anna had only recently made the cat's acquaintance. The cat had been living in the run-down shed in the side yard, keeping out of Anna's way, until Anna took a sledgehammer to the shed, unaware that any creature called it home. Fortunately, the cat had turned out to be one tough cookie, not only surviving but thriving under Anna's care. Hence her name.

"Oh, all right, you need your breakfast."

By the time Anna fed Tough Cookie and washed the cup she'd put in the sink, she could hear the first of her guests making their way down from their rooms. She helped Eoin carry his lemonade and a muffin out to the front porch, where he wriggled back into an Adirondack chair and opened a heavy book. Her mood lightened and her shoulders relaxed as she watched his red head bend down over the book, his attention immediately captured by whatever history he was reading.

Back in the front hall, she stood ready to greet each of her guests by name. Mostly couples and families visiting the town for a long weekend, they needed to know things like where to find the best spots on the beach, the best shops for beach toys, and the best cafes for lunch. Anna didn't mind spending the extra time answering their questions about Cape May and its many options for fun in the sun. She loved Cape May, loved talking about it, and loved that the B and B was—finally—fully booked for the summer.

Only one guest, a woman on her own, didn't come straight down. Anna had seen her at breakfast, so she wasn't worried. Her room was cozy and comfortable. She saw no reason Ms. Donna White wouldn't want to spend some extra time lounging around after her breakfast.

Once she'd waved her other guests off on their adventures, she turned her thoughts back to the handyman working upstairs and what he might know about the other, less-fortunate man who'd ended his days in Spicer Creek. She knew she probably shouldn't pry. Maybe it wasn't her business. Maybe he had the right to privacy, but maybe she could help.

$\mathcal{K}$ 2 $\mathcal{K}$

Anna leaned against the doorjamb and folded her arms across her chest. Luke lay on his stomach on the floor of the Harbor Room. The room was almost finished. Luke had stripped the old wallpaper, replacing it with a combination of paint and fresh paper separated by a chair rail. He'd replaced or repaired the original molding, stripped, sanded, and refinished the original wood floors, replaced all the fixtures, and completely redone the attached bathroom. Frankly, the room looked gorgeous. Now it was up to Anna to furnish and decorate it. She already had a few key pieces in mind from local shops, pieces reminiscent of a day on a yacht or sitting by the water in a cool, refreshing harbor.

At the moment, Luke did not appear to enjoy the fruits of his labor. He had a level on the floor in front of him and was eyeing the bubble indicator carefully. Two pieces of the old wood had warped, and Luke had replaced them with newer boards and carefully stained them to match.

Anna watched for a moment before speaking. She didn't mind seeing the way his back shifted as he moved the level slightly. The way his muscled legs led up to his... She shook her head. "Get a grip, Anna," she chided herself softly. Out loud, she said, "Luke, it's perfectly flat. You fixed that flaw days ago."

He grunted, rolled onto his back, and sat up. "Right. I know. Just checking."

"Uh-huh." She walked into the room, looking around at all Luke's work. "I'm super excited about this room. I love the idea of having a room decorated with boating paraphernalia."

Luke laughed. "I'm picturing the old sea shanty restaurant down at the end of the island, but I suspect that's not what you have in mind."

Anna grimaced. Of course it wasn't. This room would be elegant, refined, just like the rest of the old Victorian mansion. She hadn't given up her life in academics and moved to Cape May to open a cheesy hotel. Climbing Rose Cottage had been a classic Cape May bed-and-breakfast when her Great-Aunt Louise had run it, and it would be under Anna's ownership as well.

Luke wiped his hands down his jeans as he stood. "Did you need something?"

Anna put her hands on her hips and raised her eyebrows. "What's bugging you, Luke? I know it was something in that article. I mean, it's terrible that we have another suspicious death in Cape May, but..." She paused as she searched for the right words.

Luke let out a breath as he stowed the level in his toolbox. "Sorry. You're right." He straightened and turned to her. "I met the guy, that's all. Actually, we had an argument."

"You had an argument with the dead guy? When?"

"Before he died, obviously." Luke laughed. "It's no big deal. He was a bit of a jerk. He saw me in the hotel and thought I was a member of the staff. He wanted me to bring him fresh towels."

Anna couldn't help but laugh. How could anyone mistake Luke—with his worn denim, white T-shirt, tool belt, and toolbox—for hotel cleaning staff? "What did you do?"

Luke grinned. "At first, I just told him to find a maid. When the guy said that was my job, I told him where he could put his towels."

Anna covered her mouth with her hand. "Luke, you didn't."

He shrugged again. "What his towels are like is not my concern."

"But you're always so helpful around here. You wouldn't talk like that to one of my guests. Would you?"

"Of course not. But with you... well, you're different." He looked at her intently. "You know that."

Anna felt herself blush. "Oh. Thanks. So anyway, what happened?"

"I don't know. He stormed off, muttering something about people needing to do their jobs, that Cape May was no better than where he worked."

Luke went on about the man's complaints, but Anna had stopped listening. She hadn't heard anything after Luke mentioned the name of the university where the man worked.

"Anna?" Luke paused. "You look white. Are you okay?"

Anna put a hand against the wall and sat heavily on the wide window seat.

Luke moved to her and squatted in front of her, one hand on her leg, his eyes full of concern. "Now it's my turn to ask. What's wrong?"

She took a second then waved a hand as if to clear the air. "Sorry, it's just... the university."

"Where the guy worked?"

Anna nodded.

Luke looked confused a moment more, then his expression cleared. "Oh. Is that where you used to study?"

To say it was where she used to study was an understatement if she ever heard one. She'd dedicated all her time to that school, to her work. She'd been so close to completing her doctoral program in medical anthropology. She'd spent most of every day either in the lab or out doing her fieldwork. Her plan had been to finish her PhD then get a job in academics, where she could teach and continue her research—her plan, that was, until her lying, cheating,, academic advisor had stolen her work and published it under his own name. Her advisor who also happened to be her boyfriend.

"Right. Got it." Luke said, his voice kind. "I guess that brought up some bad memories." He stayed where he was, low in front of her, hand on her leg.

She put her hands on top of his. "I don't know why I reacted like that. I haven't thought about the place in months." *Or about my ex, Steve*, she thought to herself. "I guess it just brought back memories."

"Bad memories?"

"Hm. Not all bad. I did love my research." She looked around the room, at the home she was creating for herself, then back at Luke, one of the new friends in her life. "I miss it sometimes. You know?"

Luke nodded as he stood and held out a hand. "Come on. Let's get you back to work."

Anna took his hand with a grateful smile. "I'm sorry you had such a bad experience with Professor Oliver Humphreys-Gibbons. But I guess in the end, he had it a lot worse."

"Yeah, no kidding. So you didn't know him? From the university?"

Anna shook her head. "It's a big place. Who knows what department he was in?"

"Linguistics." When he saw Anna's surprise, Luke added, "Just one of the things he mentioned while going on about how disappointed he was."

"Right. I see. Well..." Anna considered. "I did work with folks from the linguistics department, but I never met him. My—" She cut herself off, realizing what she had been about to say. "Some of my colleagues worked more closely with the linguists. I'm sure some of them will be upset by this news."

"You were going to say something about your ex just then, weren't you?"

Anna shrugged. "What if I was? I refuse to think about him anymore. I'm really sorry to hear about Professor Humphreys-Gibbons, and I'm so sorry to know you had a bad experience with him. But this isn't about us, is it?"

"Clearly not." Luke dipped his head in agreement.

"I need to focus on my life now, not on other people's tragedies." Anna turned to leave then, on the spur of the moment, turned back and gave Luke a quick hug. "Thank you." She stepped back before she lingered in his arms too long. "For understanding."

Luke said nothing, but she felt his eyes on her as she left the room. She skipped down the stairs, knowing she had plenty of work to keep her mind off her former troubles.

The front doorbell rang just as she made it to the ground floor, so she stepped lightly to the door and flung it open. On the front porch stood her former troubles.

3

The man stood with his hands in the pockets of his khaki pants, his cotton button-down shirt open at the collar. He was looking at the ground but raised his eyes when Anna opened the door. He looked at her through the hair that fell across his deep-brown eyes. His chin was covered in a light stubble that highlighted rather than concealed his dimples. The stubble was new, he hadn't had that last time she'd seen him.

Anna took a step back and took a breath. "Steve."

"Hi, Anna." Steve Upton smiled, though his eyes kept their sad, hangdog look. "How are you?"

"Steve," Anna repeated, her hand still on the open door. "What are you doing here?"

"Can I come in?" He waved a hand toward the inside of her house.

"Anna?" Luke's voice floated down from the landing. "Everything okay?"

"You don't live here alone?" Steve asked. "That didn't take long."

Anna slammed the door shut. She spun around and stared up at Luke, crossing her hands over her chest.

"Uh-oh, what did I do now?" he asked.

She shook her head, struggling to get the words out. Luke came down as she spluttered, "Not you. No. Him. It's him."

Luke crossed the hall to the front door and opened it. Steve still stood on the porch, looking generally confused and a little amused. "Speak of the devil," Luke said. "You must be the ex."

Steve raised an eyebrow. "You were speaking of me?"

Luke grinned, but his eyes narrowed. "What are you doing here?"

"May I come in?" Steve repeated his earlier request.

Luke glanced at Anna.

She shook her head. "I'll come out."

Luke nudged the rock Anna used as a doorstop into place with his foot as Anna squeezed past him onto the wraparound porch. It was wide enough to use as an outdoor dining area in the summer months, so Anna had furnished it with not only comfortable rocking chairs and Adirondack beach chairs but also small tables and sideboards.

Choosing to keep Eoin away from this conversation, Anna stepped around Steve and headed toward the dining tables. She reached the far table then stopped. She didn't want to sit there, not in her own house, not with Steve. He wasn't welcome here.

She spun around to face him only to discover he'd followed closely behind her. She took another step back. "What do you want, Steve? Why are you here?"

Steve glanced at Luke—who stood with his arms crossed, watching them both closely—then back at Anna. As if making a decision, he frowned and lowered his eyes. "You must have heard about Oliver by now."

Anna raised her eyebrows. "Oliver? You knew Oliver Humphreys-Gibbons?"

Steve nodded, looking up at her through his hair once more. He clearly thought this was an attractive look. It wasn't. "I worked with him a few times. When I read the news, I had to come down. To see."

"To see what?" Luke asked.

Steve looked irritated by the interruption. "What? Oh. Well, to see what I could do. To help, you know? To pay my respects."

Anna frowned, suspicious of Steve's motives. "Respects? Shouldn't you wait for the funeral to do that?"

"Tell the truth, buddy. Why are you here?" Luke added.

Steve glanced once more at Luke then stepped closer to Anna.

She took a step back.

"Look, can we talk? In private?" he asked, giving Luke a meaningful glance.

"I'm not going anywhere," Luke said.

Anna took a deep breath. She had no interest in talking to Steve. Nothing good could come from it. That was for sure. But did she really want to run away from this opportunity? If she did, would she regret it? This could be her chance to prove to herself that she really was over him.

"It's okay, Luke. I'll be fine."

Luke's expression clearly said he didn't want to leave Anna with Steve, but he did as she asked. "All right. Fine. Don't forget Eoin is sitting right there, so watch what you say. And remember, I'll be right upstairs if you need me." He looked at Steve as he finished. "Just shout and I'll be right down."

As Luke pulled the front door shut behind him, a sleek black figure slipped out. Anna grinned, buoyed with the knowledge that Tough Cookie was looking out for her too.

Steve turned his eyes back to Anna. "Eoin?" He pronounced the name like Owen.

"Eoin," the boy piped up in a high-pitched voice from the other side of the porch.

"Oween," Steve repeated.

"Eoin." Eoin's voice carried disappointment, but he left it at that.

"Huh." Steve looked at Anna. "Thank you for talking with me. Now, can we go inside?"

Anna shook her head. "Nope. You want to talk, so talk."

4

Steve paced back and forth along the porch a few times before stopping with his back to Anna, his hands on the railing. He leaned forward, his head hanging low. Anna watched all of this warily, leaning back against the house, her arms folded across her chest.

She inhaled the late-morning air. It wasn't too hot yet. The June air in Cape May still carried traces of spring coolness. Birds chirped joyfully from the ancient trees lining the street. Her roses were slowly coming into their glory, pink, red, and yellow blooms spreading across the lush green leaves that climbed the trellises along the sides of the house. Tough Cookie jumped down into the flower bed below the porch, chasing an invisible critter through the hostas.

She knew Steve too well. He'd tried the sorrowful routine first, using those big brown eyes as best he could. That hadn't worked, so she steeled herself for the angry outburst that always came next. Steve blew out a loud breath and pushed himself off the rail. Anna tensed.

"Anna, I'm sorry," he said as he turned to face her, both hands held up in a gesture of penitence.

Anna straightened in surprise, her arms falling to her sides. "What?"

"I have so much to say." Steve shook his head as he clasped his hands in front of himself. "Look, if we can't go inside, can I at least buy you a cup of coffee somewhere? In town?"

Anna's eyes narrowed as she examined Steve skeptically. "What's left to say, Steve? We've been over it all before."

Steve shut his eyes as he shook his head then turned away from her again. "I know we have, but please, give me a chance to explain."

Explain? Anna needed no explanation. She opened her mouth to send him away then shut it without speaking. Was she being childish? She furrowed her brow in confusion. "All right, we can talk. But I'm not breaking bread with you somewhere. We can walk and talk." She held up a hand as Steve started to object. "That's my offer. Take it or leave it."

He examined her face then nodded. "Fine. Lead the way."

She glanced at Eoin as she stepped off the porch. He nodded slightly as he slid from his chair, leaving his book on its seat, and went inside, presumably to tell Luke about the change in plans.

Anna didn't think too much about where she was headed, she just started walking. At the corner, she turned right, Steve sticking a little too close for comfort. She picked up her pace, her mind turning in circles, trying to figure out why Steve was there—what he really wanted.

"Will you ever forgive me?" he asked, his voice close to her right ear.

She veered to her left, but the narrow sidewalk provided little wiggle room. "No."

"Ah." Steve let the word out on a breath. "I see."

They passed the Cape May branch of the county library on their left, the low building looking bright and inviting in the morning sun. A neighbor waved to her as he entered the library. Anna smiled and waved back. Then she remembered who she was walking with and dropped her hand. She definitely did not want the town gossip mill picking up on her chat with Steve.

"I've been keeping busy," Steve continued. "Still working on my research."

Anna glared at him. "*Your* research?"

"Right. Have you revisited any of your work?"

God give me strength, she thought. "I've been a little busy recently, Steve. You might have noticed the house."

"Yes, of course." They walked another block before Steve continued. "So, I'm developing a new model to explore the connections between the decisions people make about their health, how they talk about it, and the meaning they assign to societal roles."

"Mm-hm," Anna said without particular interest. Not that she didn't enjoy the topic. She would love to hear more about the work's progression. The idea that her research could help poor communities ultimately improve their health had driven her interest for so many years. It was the person delivering the information that failed to hold her interest.

After another block, Anna instinctively turned left. A block ahead, she saw Wendy Hodgson outside her kitchenware store, setting up an outdoor display of copper pots and pans, artfully presenting them along with bright-red-and-white-checked napkins and tablecloths. Wendy saw her and waved.

Oh no, Anna thought. She waved but crossed the street and turned back. Wendy was a good friend, but even so, Anna had no interest in introducing her to Steve.

"Isn't the annual conference going on right now?" Anna interrupted another of Steve's anecdotes about his ongoing research. "I know they're meeting in Philadelphia this year. I'm surprised you're not there."

"Oh, right." Steve raised his eyebrows. "I'm surprised you knew that."

"Are you kidding?" Anna's anger rose. "What, you think that just because I moved down here for a while I suddenly lost all interest in anthropology? I'm still an anthropologist, Steve. Just like you."

"Well, maybe..."

Anna glared at him again, and he promptly shut his mouth.

After a few steps, he opened it again. "No, since you ask, I'm not at the conference this year. I decided not to register. I have nothing to present, you know."

"Uh-huh. No other research you're interested in hearing about? No one presenting anything good?"

"Well, of course I'll be missing out. Brad Atherton has been doing some fascinating work. Oh—" Steve cut himself off.

"What?"

"It's just that Brad was working closely with Oliver."

"Oliver Humphreys-Gibbons?" Anna recalled the description of Oliver's corpse in the news that morning and frowned. "Oh dear."

"Yes, quite." Steve looked ahead of them to where the town's main shopping street began.

As they reached the corner, Anna briefly considered which way to turn. The pedestrianized main street ran to their left. It would lead them on a pleasant walk past restaurants, cafes, and stores, crossing a few small streets until it ended at the Magic Shop, a store run by another friend. She turned right.

She wanted to keep their walk short and sweet. She didn't want to introduce Steve to any friends or neighbors, didn't want to explain who he was or why he was there. Though she still didn't know why he was there.

A familiar-looking woman came toward them, and it took a second for Anna to recognize her solo guest, Donna White. At least she'd finally made it out of the house. She nodded a greeting but didn't stop as they passed. Steve, on the other hand, stopped walking to stare after the woman.

"Steve?"

"What?" He looked at her, his eyes vague. "Do you know Tara Blanch?"

"What? Who?" Anna wrinkled her brows in confusion then shook her head as her thoughts moved back to the world of anthropology. "Was Oliver supposed to be presenting at the anthropology conference with Brad Atherton? It seems weird that he'd be in Cape May if he was supposed to be in Philly."

"Brad mentioned that he'd be presenting. That's all. There's substantial interest in his work, you know. He's very well respected." Steve smirked, and Anna could tell he was somehow proud of the idea that a well-respected academic would talk to him about his work.

Typical.

"He didn't say anything about Oliver specifically," Steve continued. "I just assumed they'd both be there, since they worked together. I'm surprised Tara's here too."

"Who's Tara?"

A cloud of confusion passed over Steve's eyes, then he grinned. "You don't know? Ha. No one, never mind. It's no big deal. Just someone else who would've gone to the conference but apparently chose to follow Oliver instead."

"But you didn't plan to go?" Anna's skepticism quickly returned. "It had nothing to do with the fact that you figured people would shun you? Everyone knows you published research that didn't belong to you under your own name."

"Anna, how many times do I have to tell you? I based that analysis on my own work. You didn't know I was doing it."

She stopped and glared at him. She really didn't want to have this conversation. Again. "I know my own research, Steve."

"Yes, but you didn't know what I was doing. It happened to overlap with your work."

"Overlap? Your research overlapped with mine about as much as the Atlantic Ocean overlaps with Montana!" She realized she was shouting and took a breath to calm herself.

They had just passed the Methodist church. Anna had been thinking they could take the next right and work their way around the block back to Climbing Rose Cottage, but she realized now they wouldn't make it that far.

"Anna, please don't. We've been down this road. I came here..." Steve paused.

"Yes? Why did you come, Steve?"

"Well, as I said, I heard of Oliver's death. And I knew you were here. I thought we could... well, maybe talk. Maybe..."

"Maybe?" Anna's voice rose again, but she didn't care. "Maybe put it behind us? Get back together? You are insane, Steve Upton, if you think I would give you another chance. You lying, stealing, cheating, lying..." She knew she was repeating herself, so she bit her lip, her nostrils flaring as she glared at him.

"Fine. I can see that you're still angry. Perhaps I misjudged the timing." Steve sniffed and looked around. "I'll be in town for another day or so. Maybe I'll see you around."

Anna watched as Steve continued along Washington Street the way they had been walking. *How dare he? How could he?* Tears formed in her eyes, and she spun around, shutting her eyes tight. He had no right to be there, no right to butt into the new life she'd built for herself.

"Anna, are you okay?"

She opened her eyes, and a stray tear slipped down her cheek. "Minister Woodley. Hi." She wiped a hand across her eyes and smiled at the minister.

"I couldn't help but notice that you seem upset, dear. Can I help with anything?" Minister Woodley stood just outside the door of the church but moved as if to come closer.

"No, no. Thank you." Anna held up a hand. "I'm fine, really. I just need to walk this off, that's all." As much as she loved the idea of getting a pep talk from her favorite minister, she knew that if she let herself, she would break down in tears. And she had no intention of letting Steve Upton get to her like that again.

Steeling her emotions and firming her lips, she waved to Minister Woodley and focused on the sidewalk in front of her. She just needed to take one step at a time. Eventually, she would get back to the safety and comfort of Climbing Rose Cottage.

"Anna." Someone else called her name. She balled her fists at her sides. Now what?

❦   5   ❦

"Anna. Oh." Patrolman Evan Burley jogged to catch up with her but stopped when he saw her face. "What's wrong?"

Evan stood over six feet tall, and though at five foot eight Anna was hardly petite, he had to lower his head to look her closely in the eyes. His broad shoulders hunched forward, and he rested his hands on his police uniform belt.

Anna laughed and threw up her hands. "What could possibly be wrong? No, I'm sorry." She wiped her eyes again and smiled at Evan. "I'm fine. I just had a rough encounter, that's all."

Evan glanced over his shoulder, and Anna saw Jerome Walsh, Cape May's detective, following slowly.

Evan stepped close to her, blocking her view of Detective Walsh, and put a hand on her arm. He smelled like he had just come out of the shower, clean with a hint of pine. Even his uniform seemed crisp and freshly laundered. "I'm sorry. Can I do anything to help? Do you want to talk about it?"

Anna shook her head. "Nothing to talk about. My ex-boyfriend just dropped by to start a fight."

Evan raised his eyebrows, but as he started to speak, Detective Walsh joined them.

"Ms. McGregor. Anna." Detective Walsh greeted her. "It's a pleasure to see you again. I believe we might be headed in the same direction."

Anna greeted him, and the three turned to continue along Washington Street toward Ocean Street. Evan and Anna led the way, Detective Walsh following close behind.

"We need to talk with Luke," Evan explained. "I just called him, and he said he's at Climbing Rose Cottage."

Anna nodded, glancing over her shoulder and wondering why having Detective Walsh right behind her made her nervous. She could feel his dark eyes on her and imagined his pinched expression. Once again, he'd dressed without bothering to match his tie with his suit, without concerning himself with the bulge his notebook made in his jacket pocket.

She turned her thoughts back to the man at her side. "Yep. He's still working on the house. You know that."

Evan nodded, his deep-brown eyes on the road ahead of them. "Yeah, I know he spends a lot of time there."

Anna grinned and dropped her voice. "Jealous?"

As soon as she said it, she regretted it. She and Evan had never really talked about their relationship. He'd never even asked her out on a date, but they clearly had something between them, something that lit a spark in her heart every time she saw him. Even as she fumed over her encounter with Steve.

"Sorry, I'm just kidding," she said quickly. "I guess I'm still upset about having to talk with Steve."

"Yeah, what was that about? Why'd he come down from Philly?"

Anna shook her head and let her bewilderment show. "I have no idea. He said he came down to pay his respects to the man who just died. It seems he knew him."

"I'm not trying to eavesdrop or anything," Detective Walsh interrupted. "Someone you know came to town because of the death of Oliver Humphreys-Gibbons?"

"That's right." Anna turned to look at Detective Walsh. "Or at least, that's what he told me."

"And you don't believe him?" Walsh asked in a sharp voice.

"Oh. Well... I just wonder."

Walsh raised his eyebrows as if waiting for more, but Anna wasn't sure what else to add.

They reached Climbing Rose Cottage, and Anna took advantage of their arrival to change the topic. "Luke is probably upstairs." She unlocked the front door, using the keypad she'd had installed.

"I see you're taking security a little more seriously now." Detective Walsh nodded approvingly at the lock.

"Yeah. After last time..." Anna grimaced and moved into the house, calling out for Luke.

"In here." Luke's voice carried from the mudroom beyond the kitchen.

The three of them trooped through the lounge and kitchen toward the mudroom. As Anna gestured for Detective Walsh to lead the way, Evan put a hand on her arm, pulling her back slightly.

"I'm sorry Steve upset you. Did he really come down because of Oliver Humphreys-Gibbons's death?"

Anna shook her head. "That's what he said, but then he wanted to talk about his research, his life... as if we hadn't even broken up, as if nothing had changed."

She glanced into the mudroom, where Detective Walsh

formally shook Eoin's hand, Luke's green eyes watching the detective closely.

"First he said he was sorry, but when I reminded him that he hurt me, he got all upset and tried to defend himself." She shook her head and looked back at Evan.

"I get it. That's got to be tough. I hope he didn't upset you by talking about this murder."

"Murder?" Anna's eyebrows shot up. "So it is another murder?"

One side of Evan's mouth turned up in a half-grin. "A man found dead on the banks of a river? Yeah, that could be a murder. But it has nothing to do with you this time, at least." He smiled then frowned when she didn't respond. "Right?"

"Absolutely, and thank goodness." Anna nodded. "Shouldn't we...?" She bent her head toward the mudroom.

"You've been working at Congress Hall, Mr. Arnold," Detective Walsh was saying as they entered.

"That's right." Luke leaned back against the utility sink, but the room still seemed crowded. The three large men and one small boy filled the small space with an inordinate amount of masculinity. Anna pressed herself against a wall, her arms folded in front of her, in an attempt to take up less room.

"We heard you may have had an interaction with the victim of a recent crime," Detective Walsh continued.

Luke shook his head. "I should've known you'd be around to talk to me. Yeah, that's right. I spoke with a guest. I didn't know his name at the time. I recognized the description from the news this morning."

Luke's eyes fell on Anna as he spoke, and Detective Walsh turned toward her as if just realizing she was there. "Perhaps we could find somewhere more comfortable to talk."

"You're taking me in for questioning? Again?" Luke's voice carried the shock Anna felt.

"No, no, nothing like that." Detective Walsh raised a calming hand. "Perhaps we could find a seat somewhere in the house?" He turned to Anna.

"Of course. Use the lounge." She gestured toward the route they'd just followed.

Detective Walsh nodded, and he and Evan led the way. Luke glanced at Anna and rolled his eyes as he let her leave the mudroom ahead of him.

She felt his breath against her ear as he whispered, "Another murder, another chance for the cops to question me."

She suppressed a giggle. It wasn't funny.

"I'm just glad you're not involved this time," Luke continued in his low tone, unknowingly echoing Evan's earlier sentiment.

"Right," she whispered. "Right."

$$\approx \quad 6 \quad \approx$$

nna kept her head bent low over the dough as she kneaded. She had tied her mass of curly red hair back into a long ponytail. A headband kept the shorter curls off her face. She'd made the scones enough times she didn't need to think about what she was doing. Instead, she concentrated on the voices coming from the lounge.

She hadn't been invited to join the men as they took their seats to discuss what Luke knew or didn't know about Oliver Humphreys-Gibbons. They didn't seem to care when Eoin climbed up onto the window seat and pulled out his notebook. But they were in her house, interviewing her handyman and—she could add—her friend. Of course she would want to hear what they had to say.

No one had noticed her push the cat's bowl with her foot, moving it so it jutted out beyond the edge of the door. No one had noticed, either, that due to the cat bowl, the swinging door stayed ajar rather than closing firmly behind Anna when she returned to the kitchen. Now, she stood at the counter next to the door, continuing on with her regular tasks but listening closely to the interrogation in the next room.

Interrogation might be too strong a word. If that was how Detective Walsh questioned all his suspects, she had to wonder how he ever caught anyone.

Detective Walsh's tone was one of interest and concern, nothing more. "Start from the beginning. You were in the hallway, and the victim approached you?"

"That's right." Luke's voice sounded tired, as if he were already bored of going over the story.

Anna knew that was simply his way of hiding his nerves. He was savvy enough to know it wasn't a good thing to have argued with a murder victim just before the crime.

"Luke." A smile crossed Anna's face when she heard Evan's soft voice. "We're just trying to learn as much as possible about Oliver's whereabouts on the day he died. Anything you can tell us will help."

"Right. Sure." Luke let out a breath, and Anna heard the slap of his hands against his legs. "So, I was in the hallway, heading back to the part of the building I'm working on. I heard someone calling, but I didn't know he was calling me."

"What did he say?" Detective Walsh asked.

Luke paused then said, "Something like, 'Hey you?' I don't remember exactly, but I guess he had to call a few times before I turned around. Then he said, 'Finally, I've been calling.' I said, 'Sorry, I didn't realize. What can I do for you?' He said, 'I need clean towels in my room.' I said, 'You'll have to ask a maid for that.' He asked, 'Well, don't you work here?' I said, 'Yeah, but I'm a contractor. I'm not part of the regular staff.' He got all huffy and started saying things about me being rude. That's about it."

Anna heard the scratch of Detective Walsh's pen on his notebook. She couldn't imagine how much he could write.

Luke's description of the conversation had not been exactly detailed, and Anna wondered why Luke wasn't more forthcoming about the man's attitude. Although in her opinion, it was crazy they were even talking to Luke. He hadn't known the man. And a small argument—not even really an argument, just a rude encounter—hardly amounted to motive for murder. Luke would never kill anyone. Surely Evan knew that by now. The two men had ended up spending some time with each other through their connection with Anna. They weren't exactly close friends, but even so, Evan couldn't suspect Luke of murder.

After a few more seconds of silence, Detective Walsh said, "Tell me about the man. What was he wearing? Did he mention where he was going? Did he mention anyone else?"

Anna formed the dough in the pan, cutting it into triangular pieces and sprinkling sugar over the top. At least Detective Walsh asked some reasonable questions. Maybe Luke had seen or heard something helpful.

"Nothing," Luke said. "I mean," he laughed out loud. "Not that he was wearing nothing, he didn't say anything. He was dressed like... like a professor, I guess—slacks, white button-down shirt, tan linen jacket."

"So he was dressed well?"

"Yeah, I guess you could say that. He looked clean. Neat. Ha! He wore loafers with no socks. Does that help?"

"Maybe. You said he muttered something under his breath as he walked away. What else did you hear?"

"He mentioned his university, how no one could be trusted to do their job anymore, that sort of thing. Um..."

Luke paused, and Anna paused in her actions, not wanting to miss anything.

"He said he had enough to deal with already. He didn't need unreliable staff. Yeah, I know," Luke added.

Evan or Detective Walsh must have made a face at that. Probably Evan.

"What else was he dealing with, do you suppose?" Detective Walsh asked.

"I don't know. Oh, he said he was late. That must mean something, right? He looked at his watch and said, 'Damn, now I'm late.'"

"Late," Detective Walsh said. "That's another point. This was in the evening, you said, right?"

"That's right. I shouldn't even have been there that night. I just dropped by to pick up the tools I'd left."

"You don't usually work at that time of night?"

"Not unless it's an emergency, and this wasn't an emergency. Like I said, I'd left my tools there. I stopped by to grab them, and this guy insulted me. I didn't need that."

"No, of course not. So it was after eight o'clock at night, and he was running late. He was dressed well but in a casual style. Think hard, Mr. Arnold. Did he make any comment at all that might give us a clue as to where he was going?"

Luke didn't respond, but Anna imagined him shaking his head.

"All right, thank you. But please, let me know if you remember anything else."

Anna heard chairs shifting as the men stood. She pushed the scones into the oven, set the timer, and grabbed a dishcloth. She wiped her hands off as she entered the lounge, but Detective Walsh and Evan were already heading to the front door.

"Luke, you okay?" she asked.

"Yeah, fine. Seriously, it's no big deal. I'm going to get back to work." Luke headed back to the mudroom, so Anna trotted over to the front door to say bye to Evan.

The police officers were just closing the door behind

them as she approached, and she heard their quiet conversation.

"You can't suspect Luke every time someone dies in this town," Evan said, a laugh in his voice.

Detective Walsh actually laughed, too, the first time Anna had ever heard him do so. "No, of course not. But seriously, why is that man always involved when someone is murdered?"

❦   7   ❧

Anna let the front door close and leaned against it. What a relief. A poor man was dead, of course, and that was tragic. But at least this time she and Luke weren't suspects.

Her positive mood clouded as she thought about Detective Walsh's last comment. It had been a joke, clearly, she tried to convince herself. Though it did ring true. Why hadn't Luke been willing to share more about his interaction with Oliver? And why was he so eager to make sure she stayed out of it?

"Everything okay, Anna?"

She jumped at the sound of Luke's voice. "Absolutely. You'll be glad to know I just overheard Evan and Detective Walsh saying they don't think you were involved."

"Okay. Good. But they already told me that."

"Oh, right." Anna stood up straight, trying to hide the disbelief she feared was written on her face. They told Luke they didn't suspect him, and he simply believed them? Did he have no idea how the police worked?

"Look, I'm heading back upstairs. Yell if you need me,

okay?" Luke watched her closely, a curious expression on his face. "You're sure you're all right?"

Anna laughed lightly. "I'm great, Luke. Couldn't be better. At least all that nonsense took my mind off... well, you know who."

"Hey, that's right. There is a silver lining." Luke flashed his sly grin then made his way back upstairs.

Spirits raised, Anna finished her baking, cleaned up the kitchen, then grabbed Eoin and headed for Washington Mall. The famous pedestrianized street housed blocks of stores that offered something for everyone, from indulgent fudge to skinny bikinis. She followed the same path she'd taken earlier that morning with Steve, but this time she walked slowly, allowing herself to enjoy the atmosphere of Cape May in June. Eoin trotted along next to her, chatting away. Sometimes she missed the early days, when he'd been afraid to talk to her.

She waved to neighbors as she passed and stopped to chat with Wendy at her kitchen goods store. Wendy didn't ask about her earlier companion, thank goodness, because Anna had no interest in reliving that meeting.

From Wendy's store, Anna's path took her past a cozy tea shop tucked a little bit back from the street, its front yard decorated with potted plants and small candlelit tables. A favorite with locals as much as visitors, the shop offered a comfortable place to relax or a romantic enclave for a tête-à-tête. In fact, Anna noticed a couple occupying the table most hidden by the lush greenery. She smiled at the thought of a couple taking advantage of the beautiful day to have a romantic break. She barely glanced at them as she passed, fully intending to allow them the privacy they obviously wanted.

But that one glance was enough. She would know the back of that head anywhere. She'd spent too many years with him not to know every inch of him. She stumbled and had to put out a hand to catch herself.

"Cousin Anna, are you okay?" Eoin interrupted his flow of chatter and gave her a worried look.

"I'm fine." Anna took the hand he offered her. "Sorry, I just tripped."

Eoin's brows took a second to return to normal, and he looked around. Anna couldn't tell if he recognized Steve. He had his back to them, after all, and Eoin had only seen him briefly that morning. On the other hand, Eoin would recognize the woman with him just as easily as she had.

Steve Upton was having a romantic tea with Carole—or Coral, as she preferred to be called—the same woman who insisted that Great-Aunt Louise had been a busybody and detriment to the town, the same woman who thought Climbing Rose Cottage wasn't worth the time Anna was putting into it.

"Cousin Anna?" Eoin had to interrupt himself again. "Will you?"

"Will I?" Anna realized she hadn't heard a word Eoin had said. "I'm sorry, honey. I wasn't listening. What did you ask?"

Eoin's mouth tightened into a frown, but he repeated, "I'd very much like to see the new exhibit at the Community Center. They have old photographs of Cape May, and you know I've been reading about the history..."

Eoin continued in that vein until they reached Bric-N-Brac. The small bell over the door tinkled to alert the owners of their arrival. Anna had already checked out her options at this antiques-slash-odds-and-ends store run by Jacob and Emily Ahava and knew they had a number of items that would fit perfectly into her vision for the Harbor Room.

Emily Ahava greeted Anna and Eoin effusively from

where she stood behind the register. Anna explained her interests while Eoin entertained himself with the set of small wooden animals that traipsed across the windowsill.

Emily had no trouble understanding exactly what Anna was looking for. "Ah, yes, to make someone feel as if they were on a yacht or sitting in a restful harbor, looking out at the ocean, sipping a cold drink." Emily closed her eyes as she imagined the scene, perhaps picturing a harbor in her native Norway. "Then, you want brass items, yes?"

"Exactly. And mahogany. And maybe some nautical stripes." Anna nodded enthusiastically. "I know you have those old oars. I'd love to mount them on the wall."

"Oars on a wall?" Jacob Ahava came in from the back room. "That is not how they are usually used." He lowered his brows, but the twinkle in his eyes gave him away.

Emily slapped him lightly on the arm. "Of course not. Now, what else can we provide to Anna for her Harbor Room?"

"Harbors, eh?" Jacob rubbed his chin with one hand. "Boats..."

"Ah." Emily raised a finger. "That bed." She added a few words in a language Anna couldn't follow, but Jacob nodded as she spoke. Emily turned back to Anna. "We have an old brass bed frame. We can pick that up for you. Great discount." She frowned. "It might need some special attention."

"No problem." Anna waved away the concern. "I've already renovated one brass bed frame. I can do another. And you're right. That would fit well."

"There is the clock." Jacob pointed across the room, and Anna's gaze followed his finger.

"The mantel clock? Again, perfect." She squeezed between the heavily laden shelves to get to the clock, picking it up and examining it for any unfixable flaws. "I love it."

Over the next few minutes, the three of them identified more items either already available in the store or that the couple could acquire for Anna: blue-and-white-striped burlap for curtains and cushion covers, lockers that could be used as wardrobes, an old traveling trunk with drawers.

"And definitely this set of candlesticks." Anna added the items to those already on the counter next to the register.

"Ooh, perfect," Emily cooed.

"How about this antique compass?" Jacob asked. "Not functional, I must warn you. But if you are using it for decoration only...?"

"I love it," Anna said then gestured to an item against the wall. "Now that wicker bench would look perfect as a window seat."

Her selections made and delivery dates scheduled for the larger items, they set to work on agreeing on a final price. Haggling had never been Anna's strong suit, but she knew she could trust the Ahavas. While they enjoyed a bit of arguing over the cost, they always ultimately agreed to a price that was more than fair. Anna was thrilled with how far she could spread her limited budget in their store.

"Terrible news about that poor man." Emily put the smaller items into a shopping bag. "Did you read about that?"

"I did." Anna avoided Emily's eyes. She knew the kind of reputation she'd earned in town last time a murder had been committed and didn't want to encourage that.

"In Spicer Creek, was it not?" Jacob shook his head. "Strange, that."

"Strange? Terrible, I think. For someone to die, to be found washed up in Spicer Creek." Emily shuddered then paused and looked sideways at her husband. "Why do you say strange? Are you thinking of the other...?"

Jacob nodded as he raised one eyebrow.

"But that was so long ago," Emily said.

"What other?" Anna looked back and forth between the Ahavas.

"How long ago?" piped up Eoin, who had joined Anna at the register.

"Oh, about fifty years ago. Before our time," Jacob replied, chuckling.

"But it is odd, no?" Emily asked. "Another body in the same place."

"There was another body?" Eoin's eyes grew wider than normal, his mouth opening into an O.

"In the same place?" Anna rested a hand on Eoin's shoulder, pulling him close to her. "That's terrible."

Emily widened her eyes at Eoin. "They say the ghost of that poor man still haunts the canal."

"Nonsense." Jacob scoffed. "Don't listen to her, young man, and don't be scared. Ghosts don't exist."

Emily grinned wickedly. "But it does entice the tourists. Doesn't it?"

Anna had to agree with that. "It's true. Ghost tours, ghost stories, they all sell tickets. But why did you think of that death from so long ago?"

Jacob shrugged. "A dead body in the same place simply seemed odd to me."

Emily nodded. "Spooky, even. What if they're connected?"

"How could they be?" Anna asked. "You said that happened more than fifty years ago."

Emily shrugged. "You know what they say about Cape May's connection to the past."

Her tone was serious, but Anna saw the twinkle in her eyes.

"It's not spooky. It's tragic." Anna corrected her gently, mostly for Eoin's benefit. "He's not just a body. He's a man—Oliver Humphreys-Gibbons, professor at my former school, in fact."

"Oh no, my dear. I'm so sorry." Jacob extended a hand toward Anna. "Was he your friend?"

"No, nothing like that." Anna shook her head. "I'm fine, really. I just wanted…"

She glanced down at Eoin, and Emily nodded.

"Of course, dear. I completely understand." She passed the few bags over to Anna and reminded her of the delivery date for the larger items.

Despite the scheduled delivery, Anna and Eoin both had their hands full when they left the store. As they passed the Magic Shop, Anna was tempted to pick up some dried flowers and candles, but the weight of her bags and the view of Eoin struggling to hold a bag almost as big as him convinced her to wait for another time.

They had just turned onto Perry Street, heading back toward the beach and Climbing Rose Cottage, when a car slowing behind them caught her attention. She turned to see a police cruiser pulling in beside the Magic Shop, Evan behind the wheel. Detective Walsh stepped out before the car had come to a complete stop.

Why were the police at the Magic Shop? As tempted as she was to hang around to watch, she knew it wouldn't be the right thing to do—or a good influence for Eoin.

"Come on," she called to the boy, who had turned to watch as well. "We're going home."

8

Anna was on the third floor, depositing her purchases, when the doorbell rang. Her guests had the code to unlock the door themselves, and she didn't expect anyone new today. She jogged down the two flights of stairs and peered through one of the narrow, curtained windows that bracketed the door then flung the door open.

"Brooke, what a nice surprise. Come in." She stepped back and gestured for the young woman who stood on her porch to enter.

Anna had met Brooke Cortinas only six weeks earlier when Anna had stopped by the store Brooke ran with her uncle. Since that first meeting, Anna had dropped by Brooke's shop whenever she could, and they had even managed to go out for coffee a few times.

On the surface, the two women didn't look like they would have much in common. Where Anna was tall and athletic, with a mane of red hair and the naturally white complexion that came with it, Brooke was shorter, carried a few extra pounds, and wore her black hair cut into an angular bob that slid forward and covered her face. When Anna chose to wear makeup—which wasn't often—she limited herself to lipstick and mascara. Brooke, on the other hand, never went without the dark lines painted around her eyes in shapes that brought ancient Egyptian priestesses to mind.

Despite their superficial differences, they had a lot of similarities. They were both twentysomething women who managed their own business—well, in Brooke's case, she managed her uncle's business—and shared a love for Cape May and their own roles in the thriving beach town. They'd joined the local small business association together and enjoyed sharing notes, the good and bad.

"It's great to see you, Brooke." Anna followed Brooke into the lounge. "I'm so glad you're here. I've been wanting to show you Climbing Rose Cottage."

Brooke looked around, the silver rings in her nose and eyebrow catching the morning light streaming through the wide windows. "It's a gorgeous house, Anna. It looks like you've done a great job fixing it up. The garden is thriving."

"I don't know about that." Anna slipped onto the couch and gestured for Brooke to do the same. "It's not as healthy as when Aunt Louise managed it, but I'm getting there."

"Have you...?" Brooke's voice caught. She covered her mouth with a hand while she coughed, then continued. "Have you finished going through your great-aunt Louise's things yet?"

"Not yet, no." Anna narrowed her eyes, her forehead furrowing. "I'm taking my time with that. It's kind of tough, you know? But why do I get the sense you didn't come here to see the house? Or talk about Great-Aunt Louise?"

Brooke shook her head, stood, and moved about the room. She paused in front of the bookshelf, examining the titles. Then she moved across to the low shelf near the window, picking up one of the small porcelain figures on display there. It was a woman dressed for a party in the nineteenth century, her long gown tight against her body except for the bump of her bustle. It was a beautiful figurine, though not one Anna would have picked out herself. Brooke turned to Anna with a question in her eyes.

"Great-Aunt Louise's," Anna answered the unspoken question. "She had a whole collection of them. I found them in her rooms when I finally went through them. I figured they were beautiful, and they match the style of the house, so I put a few out on display."

Brooke lifted one side of her mouth and put the figurine down with exaggerated care. "Your great-aunt Louise had very good taste, Anna. I need to do some research, but I think those might be valuable."

"Really?" Anna jumped up and came over to the window.

Brooke stepped away as soon as Anna approached, keeping her back to Anna.

Anna watched her wander for a moment more then said, "Brooke, what's wrong?"

Brooke sighed loudly and threw herself back down on the sofa. She leaned forward, elbows on her knees, and buried her face in her hands, her shoulders shaking.

"Oh, Brooke." Anna ran to sit next to her, wrapping her arms around Brooke's shoulders. "Oh, honey, what's wrong? What can I do?"

Brooke didn't look up as she answered, and her tears and hands covering her face muffled her words. "They arrested Uncle Lorenzo."

Anna's eyes opened wide, and she leaned in closer to hug Brooke. Why would the police arrest Uncle Lorenzo? Anna had only met him a couple of times, but he seemed harmless. A little quirky, perhaps, and Anna suspected he was not the sort to worry much about strictly adhering to the letter of the law. She was pretty sure the incense she often smelled wafting from the back office was intended to cover up other activities. But no one got arrested for smoking a little pot, did they?

She rubbed her friend's back. "Talk to me, Brooke. What happened? Why was he arrested?"

Brooke looked up. The carefully painted black lines around her eyes ran in rivulets down her face and around her lips. Anna grabbed a box of tissues from the shelf across the room, then returned to continue comforting Brooke.

Brooke took an ineffective swipe at her face with a tissue then blew her nose loudly before grabbing a few more tissues. It took a couple of minutes, but she finally took a deep breath and looked at Anna.

"Do you feel a little better? Sometimes it helps to let it out." Anna continued to rub Brooke's back.

Brooke offered a sad smile and nodded.

"So the police arrested your uncle Lorenzo?"

"Well, not exactly," Brooke shook her head. "They said they were just taking him in for questioning, but you know what that really means."

Anna nodded, thinking of Luke's innocence. "I do. I really do."

"And the weirdest part, Anna... the worst part—" Brooke sniffed and grabbed another tissue. "He wasn't even surprised when they turned up. He acted like he was expecting them."

"Well, maybe he did something recently that he knows he shouldn't have done?" Anna tried to ask the question gently, but even as she spoke, she knew she couldn't take the sting out of her words.

"No way!" Brooke jumped up. "He didn't do it!"

"Sorry, sorry. I should have waited to hear more before I said anything." Anna stood, too, and rested her hands on Brooke's arms. She looked her in the eye. "Tell me. What did they want to question him about?"

Brooke sniffed one more time then looked Anna square in the eye. "They think he murdered that man."

9

"Now, start from the beginning." Anna handed Brooke a steaming cup of vanilla tea.

After Brooke's outburst, Anna had calmed the young woman and guided her into the kitchen, where Eoin was finishing off a tuna fish sandwich. Anna settled Brooke onto a stool at the high counter as Tough Cookie rubbed around Brooke's ankles, purring loudly. Eoin's big eyes—made even bigger by his round, metal-framed glasses—followed them closely.

Brooke straightened from petting Tough Cookie and accepted the tea gratefully, lowering her face toward the mug as she blew off the steam and took a sip.

"Why would the police think Lorenzo had anything to do with this stranger's murder?" Anna asked.

"And why was Uncle Lorenzo so unsurprised when they showed up?" Brooke followed up with a question of her own. She shook her head, wide-eyed. "I have no idea."

"Well, have you asked him?"

"How could I? He wouldn't even look me in the eye as he left. He just told me to stay at the store and said I'd be okay on my own." Brooke's lips quivered as she took another sip.

Anna sat heavily on the next stool and put a hand on Brooke's leg. "I'm so sorry, honey. I can only imagine how upsetting that must have been. Tell me more about Lorenzo. I've only met him a couple of times and really don't know much about him."

"Hm." Brooke took a deep breath as she raised her eyebrows. "Well... he moved here about two years ago."

"Where did he used to live?" Anna bent down to tickle Tough Cookie behind the ears.

The cat let out a rumble that sounded like a passing freight train. As she sat up, she noticed Eoin had produced his notebook and was writing furiously. Of course he was.

"He moved around a lot," Brooke answered, her gaze on the cat. "I'm not sure he's ever stayed in one place very long, at least not until he moved here to stay with me."

"He moved here to be with you?"

Brooke nodded, tears welling in her eyes once again. "I was twenty. An adult, I know, but I'd always lived with my parents. When they decided to sell the shop and move to Florida, I wasn't sure what to do."

"Why did they want to leave? And why not let you take over the shop?" Anna asked, confused.

Brooke grimaced. "They didn't trust me with it. They always treated me like I was a kid. You know how parents can be."

Anna thought of the warnings her own parents had given her when she announced her intention to take over Great-Aunt Louise's business. Her mother was convinced that twenty-six was far too young to run a B and B. "I get it. I really do."

Brooke shrugged. "Anyway, I don't want to live in Florida." She shuddered. "All old people and golf courses and..." She shuddered again.

Anna laughed. "I'm not sure that's all it is, but I get what you're saying. You wanted to stay in Cape May."

"Of course I did." Brooke leaned forward on the counter, her arms folded in front of her. "I have friends here, I have a life here, and I'm old enough to be on my own."

"But you needed a job. I assume you worked at the store for your parents?"

"Yeah, but it was a different store." Brooke finished her tea before continuing. "They ran a candy shop where I used to work."

"In the same space you're in now?"

Brooke nodded. "Yep. Right around the time they decided to move, Uncle Lorenzo was looking for somewhere new to live. The timing was perfect. They sold him the store and moved to Florida, and he moved in here with me. Thank goodness he didn't want to run a candy store." Brooke smiled again, rolling her eyes.

Anna laughed. "I love the store you run now. It's so... eclectic."

"That was all Uncle Lorenzo's idea, but I love it. It's perfect for me, for both of us. Uncle Lorenzo is a magician."

"A magician!" Anna said, surprised. "I didn't know that. I've never met a professional magician before."

"Right... well..." Brooke shifted uncomfortably on her stool. "According to my parents, it's not so easy to make a living as a magician, but Lorenzo always did okay. He sold a lot of things, I think. That's why he was perfect for the store. Now he manages the store with me and still does some magic shows, for parties, you know? So he's not... dependent on his shows."

Anna narrowed her eyes as Brooke spoke. "What are you leaving out?"

Brooke lowered her head more toward the counter, and her voice dropped. "He may have been a bit of a... well, my mom would say a con man."

"A con man?"

Brooke nodded, clearly uncomfortable. "It's not true. I'm sure of it. Or at least, if he was, he's not anymore. He loves mystery, magic, witchcraft, spells, even a little dark magic. He's not a con man. He really does believe in spirits, things we can't understand, certain powers at work. He works hard at the store, and he works hard at his magic."

Eoin's squeak reminded Anna that he was listening intently and taking notes. She should probably be more careful in the future about which conversations he was allowed to hear.

"So he opened up the Magic Shop, and it's fabulous," Anna said and meant it.

The store carried a wide selection of items designed to interest anyone curious about magic, fantasy, even witchcraft. With everything from healing herbs to dragon figurines, the store was a big hit with teenagers as well as their parents.

"He sounds like a wonderful person, Brooke. I'm so sorry you're going through this. But I'm sure everything will be fine. The police must have some reason for wanting to talk to him. Maybe Oliver Humphreys-Gibbons was in the store the other day, and you just didn't see him. They just talked to Luke this morning because Luke saw the man at his hotel."

"Really?" Brooke looked up, hope in her eyes.

"Absolutely." Anna nodded. "They probably just want to know if he saw or overheard anything that could help."

Though why they would take him down to the police station to ask him those questions Anna didn't understand.

"And what if there's more to it?" Brooke asked. "What if he is involved? I really don't know much about Uncle Lorenzo's life before he moved here. What if...?" Her voice died out with a small tremor.

"Stop it. Don't even think that. Look, your friends are here for you. I'm here for you. And if there's anything I can do, any way I can help, just ask."

Brooke smiled, but her eyes dropped. "Thank you, but there's nothing you can do. Unless you can convince the police Uncle Lorenzo wasn't involved in this murder."

10

"Don't look at me like that. You know I can't do anything." Anna refused to look at Tough Cookie, who watched her from the doorway. "Sure, I helped out last time someone died, but I had to. It was a matter of survival." She dropped the sheets she'd pulled from the bed into the hamper and finally turned to look down at Tough Cookie.

The cat continued to glare at her, even as she raised one dainty paw to lick it.

Anna rolled her eyes as she pulled clean sheets from the closet and remade the bed. She'd already cleaned the bathroom, so after a quick run-through with the duster and vacuum cleaner, she grabbed her supplies and moved to the next bedroom.

Tough Cookie followed her down the hall, watching as Anna cleaned each room, the cat's presence like a silent accusation.

Anna's frustration grew. As she moved into the last room, she dropped the hamper, put her hands on her hips, and glared back at the cat. "Believe me. I want to help. I do! I hate feeling useless—powerless—but this isn't my business."

Tough Cookie blinked.

"Ugh. What do you want me to do? Try my hand at investigating again? Remember, I almost got killed last time I stuck my nose into a murder investigation."

She swung the hamper onto her hip and moved on to clean the final room, muttering to the cat, "I am an investigator. It's true. But a scientific investigator, not a detective." She glanced over her shoulder at Tough Cookie, who sat with her head to one side. "It's not the same thing. I trace patterns of migration, following the movement of indigenous remedies, not the movements of criminals."

The bed done, she moved to the bathroom. Tough Cookie moved with her, waiting in the doorway once again, still watching. "I know how... to gather... data..." Anna grunted as she scrubbed the tub. "I know how to analyze, not solve crimes."

Even as she defended herself to the cat—an action she preferred not to dissect—her determination grew. How could she not help Brooke?

Finished with the rooms, Anna heaved the full hamper into her arms and made her way to the basement laundry. Not yet satisfied that she'd accomplished her goal, Tough Cookie twined around Anna's legs as she descended.

"Watch out!" Anna almost tripped as she barely avoided crushing the cat's tail. "Are you trying to kill me? What kind of friend are you?"

Tough Cookie raced down the stairs to the front hall and looked back up at her.

"Right. What kind of friend am I?"

She'd just pulled open the basement door, standing on one foot, her hands full and her other foot holding the door open, when the doorbell jingled. She turned to see Donna White.

"Oh, hi. Sorry," Donna mumbled, barely making eye contact. "I don't want to get in your way. I just need to... uh... grab something from my room. Is that okay?"

"Of course, of course." Anna dropped the hamper and let the basement door swing shut. "I've done all the bedrooms, so please feel free to spend as much time in your room as you'd like."

Donna nodded her thanks and strode toward the stairs.

"Are you in Cape May to see anything in particular?" Anna called out, curious about her quiet guest.

Donna paused, one hand on the bannister. She shook her head. "Not at all. Just looking for some peace and quiet." With a nod, she continued up the stairs.

Anna watched her go, wondering. She had no problem understanding why someone would come to spend a long weekend alone in Cape May. The town offered so much to see and do. It didn't necessarily require company. But it was a little odd that Donna spent so much time in her room. If Anna were her, she would spend all her days wandering along the beach, enjoying the ocean.

She felt Tough Cookie's paw on her leg. "Right. Laundry." She sighed as she lugged the hamper down to the washing machine. The cat followed her.

"I'm not off the hook yet, huh?" She sorted the sheets and shoved them into the washer. "What about the whole ghost idea? If a ghost is involved, then I can't really do anything. I'm no ghost hunter." She grinned as she closed the washing machine door and poured soap into the detergent drawer.

"Ghosts?"

Anna spun around, knowing full well that Tough Cookie couldn't possibly have said that but a little worried about her sanity nonetheless. "Eoin! How long have you been there?"

"I just came down, Cousin Anna. I was looking for you. It's been a long time since lunch, y'know."

Anna turned the washing machine on then gave her cousin a quick hug. "I hope I didn't scare you, talking about ghosts. You know there's no such thing, right?"

Eoin's forehead wrinkled. "I don't know. We don't know about a lot of things, right? And Ms. Ahava said she'd heard the stories."

"Don't let Emily Ahava trick you into believing things like that. They really are just stories."

Tough Cookie meowed and put a paw on her leg. "Though I have heard that cats can see ghosts. Can't you?" She bent down and tickled Tough Cookie's ears.

"If I go to the exhibit at the Community Center, I might see some ghosts in the old pictures." Eoin looked up at her hopefully. "Can I? Please? Please?"

Anna laughed. "Of course you can, honey. Run upstairs. I'll be up in a minute to make you a snack. Then I'll take you to the Community Center. In fact, I need to get out of the house too."

Anna dropped the sheet she was spreading over the ironing board. The ironing could wait. Tough Cookie followed her back up the stairs, twining around Anna's ankles as she climbed. She leaped up the last few steps and over the cat, then stumbled into the lounge to look for her phone.

She paused. Something was off. She turned in a circle, trying to identify what had caught her attention. What was where it shouldn't be? Or not where it should be? Her gaze finally landed on the line of female figurines. Where six women had stood in a row, now there were five with a wide gap where the missing figurine had been.

Anna walked around the sofa toward the shelf and gasped.

Shattered pieces of ceramic sprinkled the wood floor. Various-sized chunks of pink, blue, and green, with the rough white edges exposed, were all that remained of the missing figure.

How could this have happened? she wondered as she bent down to pick up the larger pieces.

Tough Cookie joined her, purring and rubbing between her legs.

"Did you do this?" She glared at the cat. "Don't try to get out of it by purring. I know Eoin wouldn't break something like this. If he had, he would have told me, and no one else has been in here."

Anna felt a pinch as Tough Cookie swatted her leg, her claws only barely poking through her jeans. "Oh right, there was Ms. White. Could it have been her?"

If it was, it must have been an accident. No guest would have a reason to break the figurine intentionally. Donna White must have been too embarrassed to report it or too cheap to pay for the damage. Anna's anger rose. What kind of guest would do such a thing? Not someone she wanted staying in her house.

Tough Cookie meowed and gently scratched her leg again.

"You're right. I can't be sure. But what else could it have been? Ghosts?" A shiver ran up and down Anna's back. "I better make that call before my imagination gets away from me."

"Cheers, ladies." Felicia Keane held up her glass of white wine. "To a beautiful June day with wonderful friends."

"Cheers." Anna raised her glass in response then turned to her right, where Sammy Shields, her best friend in the world, sat. As always, Sammy looked gorgeous. Dressed casually in khaki shorts and a pink T-shirt, Sammy nevertheless managed to look glamorous. Her strappy sandals had just enough of a heel. Her T-shirt hung loosely enough to almost expose the tops of her shoulders. Her silky blond hair practically glowed as it caught the sunlight filtering through the porch canopy under which they sat.

Too bad Eoin wasn't with them. He would have loved to see Sammy, Anna knew. But it was a good opportunity for her to meet with her friends without Eoin listening in, and he'd been so excited to spend a few hours at the Community Center.

"Thanks so much for meeting me for this late lunch." Anna placed her wine back on the table. "I have to admit, as much as I love seeing you both, I have an ulterior motive."

"Ah-hah, I should have guessed." Felicia narrowed her eyes, deepening the creases that spoke to the many years she had lived in the seaside town, years of enjoying the sun on her face, the wind in her hair. Though with the short, no-nonsense haircut Felicia preferred, Anna didn't imagine the wind affecting the woman's gray hair much.

"What? You don't think I'd want to have lunch on a gorgeous day with two of my closest friends?" Anna asked, surprised.

"No, dear, of course that's not it." Felicia leaned over and patted her hand. "It's just that I thought I saw something in your expression, a certain gleam in your eye, when I arrived."

Anna wasn't surprised. Felicia's cheerful and generous character was coupled with the sharp eyes and mind of a librarian. She was a woman who knew what to look for and where to look. She wouldn't miss a thing.

"Well, I'm just thrilled to be out of the bakery for the afternoon." Sammy watched the waiter as he placed their dishes in front of them.

The waiter, of course, let his eyes linger a little too long on Sammy. Men always did. They were easily distracted by her looks without realizing she was a hard-nosed businesswoman who ran one of the best bakeries around.

Anna's best friend since before they could walk, Sammy had opened the Wild West Bakery in West Wildwood, a town just up the beach. One of the best things about Anna's recent move to Cape May was how close she and Sammy were once more.

Anna dug into her crab-and-shrimp-cake sandwich, letting her friends enjoy their food before explaining the predicament she wanted their help with. Once they'd taken a few bites, Anna explained why she'd called them.

"Do you remember Brooke Cortinas?" she asked.

Sammy nodded as she picked a shrimp from her salad and put the whole thing in her mouth. She grinned as she chewed.

If only those men who adored her could see her now, Anna thought, laughing.

"Of course," Felicia responded, putting down her slice of pizza and dabbing at her mouth with her napkin. "She and Lorenzo run the magic store." She raised her eyebrows. "If you can call it that."

"Right… I know it's a little unusual."

"Hm." Felicia took another bite of pizza. "You could say that. I've heard rumors about him."

"Oh yes?" Sammy wiggled her eyebrows. "What kind of rumors? Do dish."

Felicia pinched her lips together and shook her head as she let out a long breath. "I assume you have a reason for the conversation, Anna, and not just rampant gossip."

"I do, I promise." Anna nodded.

"Well," the older woman continued. "The rumors are that he has a bit of a past, something illicit, perhaps—involvement in criminal activities even. I'll be honest, some of the women in town don't trust him at all."

"But his store is great," Anna said. "It's so much fun. I love browsing the shelves. You never know what you're going to find."

"Fun, yes," Felicia agreed. "Though I do worry about how many people out there take the idea of magic and witchcraft a little too far."

"That's ridiculous," Anna said. "Do they ruin the ghost tours too? It's all just a bit of fun, and the tourists love it."

"Well, now I really have to visit that store," Sammy

chimed in. "Some of the stores along Washington Street are so... I don't know, typical? Expected?"

"When tourists come to town, they want to see certain things, Sammy," Anna said. "You know how it is. In a beach town, you're going to want to buy souvenirs, maybe a painting, books..." She waved a hand in the air as if it could continue the list.

"Quite right." Felicia nodded as she spoke around her pizza. "But most of the stores are really special—don't forget Bric-N-Brac or the toy store or that amazing lingerie place." Felicia grinned wickedly, and Anna had to admit she was shocked. She hadn't expected Felicia to be a customer at that particular store.

As they finished their meals, their conversation turned to the problems, perils, and joys of having a town whose survival was tied to the tourist industry as well as the value provided to all local business by the town's small business association. Anna relaxed and enjoyed the conversation, one she'd had before and would surely have many times again. She had no doubt she'd made the right choice when she'd abandoned her studies to move to Cape May.

Felicia spoke about the library and how grateful she was that they could rely on local patrons and not depend on tourists.

"And how is the debate team doing?" Anna chimed in. "Those girls are amazing."

The local high school sponsored a debate team, and Anna had had the privilege of meeting some of the participants when they'd visited the library for their research. Their never-ending, all-consuming research.

"Oh, they're digging into everything I can find for them, as always." Felicia glanced at Sammy. "They have to be prepared to debate any topic, you see. They show up for debates without knowing the topic in advance, or even which side of the topic they have to debate. Then they get a brief interlude to prepare, and that's it. They go."

Sammy looked skeptical. "Any topic?"

"Absolutely." Anna launched into an explanation of how BethAnne, one of the girls on the team, had explained the way they worked.

The sun had shifted in the sky by the time the women finished their meal, sipped the last of their drinks, and paid their bill. They walked slowly out to the parking lot, where Sammy's car waited. Anna and Felicia intended to walk back into town.

Before heading to her car, Sammy turned toward the boat ramp at the back of the parking lot. Anna happily followed her.

"It is beautiful here." Sammy's eyes followed the path of Spicer Creek from the fancy marina to the south, along the wild banks, then north toward the Cape May canal.

Gulls called from somewhere nearby, and the purr of a big yacht's engine carried across the water as the boat made its way up toward the canal.

"We need to help Brooke," Anna said.

"You never told us what the problem was, Anna. What happened?" Sammy asked.

"The police suspect Lorenzo in the murder of that poor man who was found dead."

Sammy shuddered. "Oh. He was found here, wasn't he? In Spicer Creek?"

"Not right here, dear." Felicia put an arm around Sammy's shoulders. "Up that way, toward the canal. You wouldn't even be able to see the spot from here." She gestured toward the spot as she spoke, her finger following the path of the yacht as it passed. "Anna, why do the police suspect him?"

"I don't know. Brooke doesn't know. But she's terrified,

as you can imagine. She knows her uncle didn't kill the guy."

"Perhaps he was involved in some other way?" Felicia raised one eyebrow.

Now it was Anna's turn to shiver. She wrapped her arms around herself despite the strong afternoon sun. "Perhaps. But Brooke doesn't think so. And she knows him well enough to be sure, right?"

"Of course, of course." Felicia agreed. "But what can we do? The police are investigating a murder. They will look at every possibility. You know that."

"Sure." Sammy nodded. "If Lorenzo didn't do it, Detective Walsh will let him go. He was pretty reasonable last time."

"Yes, he was," Felicia agreed. "He's a good detective. He'll do his job."

Anna raised an eyebrow. "He certainly benefitted from our help last time someone died unexpectedly in Cape May." She shrugged. "I just thought I would ask around a bit and see if I could find anything to help Lorenzo." She looked carefully at her friends. "To help Brooke."

Anna took her paper cup of tea outside and grabbed the one empty table in front of the tea shop, sliding onto a plastic chair and looking around. The sunny afternoon had brought crowds of visitors to the town. They strolled along the waterfront street where she sat and fanned out across the beach. She could just see the tops of red, white, yellow, blue, and green umbrellas scattered along the sand beyond the dunes.

She leaned back in the chair, grateful for the narrow strip of shade created by the tea shop's overhanging roof. At this time of year, she got sunburned just by thinking about being in the sun, thanks to the pale skin that came with her bright-red hair. At least she didn't have freckles. She meant to keep it that way.

She closed her eyes, listening to the screech of the gulls and the shouts and laughs of beachgoers playing games in the sand. After lunch, she'd buckled down to the daily chores that dominated her life these days. She was grateful her B and B was fully booked, no question. Particularly after her somewhat rocky start. But a full house meant a full afternoon of chores. She'd finished it all, though, and had earned the opportunity to take some time away to enjoy the beauty of Cape May and appreciate the weather and atmosphere. And to think about murder.

"Anna." Evan's voice startled her. She opened her eyes to see the tall officer staring down at her, his own cup of tea in hand. "Sorry to make you wait."

A broad smile spread across her face, and she blushed. She really needed to learn to control her expressions around Evan. "I'm just glad you had time to meet me. I can only imagine how busy you must be right now."

Evan pulled out the other plastic chair, eying it warily before sitting carefully. It made an uncomfortable noise but held his weight. "It's true. I can't believe we have another murder to solve. I feel like we only just wrapped up that last one."

Anna grinned and raised an eyebrow. "As I recall, I was very helpful last time. Maybe I could offer my services again?" She tried to keep her tone light, knowing exactly what Evan's response would be. She wasn't wrong.

"No way." He leaned forward on the rickety table, which wobbled under his weight. "Absolutely not. Remember what happened last time? You could have been killed."

Anna toyed with the edge of her cup. "Well, that's true. But you said yourself you wouldn't have solved the case without me."

"Hm." Evan took a sip of tea. "I said that, but Detective Walsh wouldn't have agreed—if I'd even mentioned it to him, which I didn't."

Anna chewed on her lip and looked out over the ocean. Waves broke a hundred yards out from the shore, the water rolling in gently to lap at the feet of the children brave enough to take a dip in the cold water. She recalled a walk she and Evan had taken along the edge of the water, the thrill she'd felt when he'd touched her hand or put his arm around her waist. She kept her eyes on the water. "I know, Evan. I understand."

"Hm," he said again. "Why don't I believe you?"

She flashed a bright grin as she turned back to him. "Because you know me too well, clearly. Look, I won't get involved. I promise. I just told Brooke I'd find out what was going on with her uncle, Lorenzo Cortinas. You brought him in for questioning."

Evan's brow furrowed. "Lorenzo should be back at home by now. Detective Walsh interviewed him for a few hours—it's true—but the interview ended around three." Evan looked at his watch. "An hour ago."

"Oh." Anna sat forward, surprised. "I guess Brooke didn't call to tell me."

"Or he didn't go straight home," Evan pointed out. "Anyway, Brooke should talk to her uncle. She should ask him why we questioned him."

Anna raised one eyebrow. "Is he not telling her something?"

Evan scowled and put his cup down. "Anna, you know I can't talk about the case. Is that the only reason you wanted to meet for tea?"

Anna blushed. "No. It's good to see you, Evan. I know I've been busy now that people are finally booking at Climbing Rose Cottage again. I really did want to catch up."

Evan relaxed back into his chair. The wind caught his hair, mussing it around his forehead and bringing out the red highlights. "I'm glad to hear that. Tell me how it's been going."

Anna let herself enjoy the next thirty minutes, catching Evan up on her recent guests, her new involvement in the local small business association, the stories she'd heard from friends back in Philadelphia, and of course the latest gossip around Cape May. "Gossip is running pretty rampant about Lorenzo right now, as you can imagine."

"Yeah, I guess it would be. It's a tragedy, Anna." Evan shook his head. "It seems like everyone gets hurt in a murder investigation."

Anna thought back to the last—and only—time she'd been involved in a murder investigation. "That's so true. So you think it was someone local?"

Evan shrugged. "You know I can't talk about it, but I can tell you what Detective Walsh told the press. The victim didn't drown. He was strangled."

"Strangled?" Anna repeated, surprise in her voice. "But he was found in the water."

Evan nodded. "It looks like he was strangled then dumped in the water. He could have been on a boat when he was killed and pushed overboard, or walking along the creek and the killer pushed him in the water. Lots of possibilities, really."

Anna thought about this for a moment. "It must have been someone pretty strong, then, right? It's not easy to strangle someone."

"The victim was an average-size guy, not particularly big. But you're right, it was probably a man, someone with the strength to subdue the victim then hold him down long enough to wrap a rope around his neck—" Evan cut himself off. "Oh, I'm so sorry. I shouldn't have described it like that."

Anna felt the blood rushing from her face as Evan described the death so vividly. She bowed her head and thought about the life that had ended so brutally. "That's terrible," she whispered.

"I know. I'm sorry. I shouldn't have told you that."

She waved a hand and looked back up at him. "I'm okay. But who was this guy, Oliver Humphreys-Gibbons? I know he taught at my old university. I told you Steve said he knew the guy. But I mean, what happened to him that someone would attack him like that?"

Evan shrugged. "That's what we need to find out. And by we, I mean the police. Right?" He lowered his head to stare directly into her eyes.

"Of course," she mumbled into her tea, not meeting his eyes.

Anna settled back into her couch, a bowl of cereal in her hands. *The dinner of champions*, she laughed to herself. She'd finished cleaning up after her afternoon tea service. Despite the fact that bed-and-breakfasts traditionally only offered breakfast—much as the name implied—those in Cape May had taken to providing some kind of late-afternoon service as well. The offerings varied by B and B, each focusing on what they did best. For Anna, that meant late-afternoon tea and cookies, with dry sherry for those who wanted it.

Eoin had eaten his dinner while her guests had their tea. He'd come home starving—not unusual in an eight-year-old boy, Anna suspected—and inhaled two servings of macaroni and cheese. By the time she'd cleared everything away and finished all the prep work for breakfast the next morning, Anna was too tired to worry about her own dinner, so cereal it was.

She stuck the spoon in her mouth as she picked up her phone to call Sammy.

"Hey, friend, what's cooking?'

Anna couldn't help but smile when she heard Sammy's voice. "Hey, Sammy, you sound tired."

"Me? I was just going to say that about you. Tough day, huh?"

Anna could hear Sammy moving around her apartment as she talked, a chair sliding across the floor, a drawer opening and closing. "I guess. It was great to see you, though. That helped. But listen, I forgot to tell you something. I can't believe I forgot. Maybe it's a good thing, since it means I wasn't dwelling on it—"

Sammy cut her off. "It would be easier for me to know whether it was good if you started by telling me what it is."

"Right." Anna yawned then heard Sammy yawn on the other end of the line. "I saw Steve today."

It took Sammy a moment before she responded. "You saw Steve?" Her voice flattened in disbelief.

Anna nodded as she finished a spoonful of cereal. "Mm-hm. He came by. Just knocked on my door. I opened it, and there he was."

"Wow. That man has some nerve. Did you punch him?"

Anna laughed. Why hadn't she talked to Sammy about this earlier? What a crazy day it had been. "I wanted to, believe me. He wanted to come in and have me serve him coffee while he chatted about his research."

As she spoke, Tough Cookie jumped up next to her onto the couch, headbutting her in a request for attention. Anna lifted the cat onto her lap, holding her cereal bowl higher and out of the way.

"What? You didn't though, right?"

"Of course not." Anna grimaced. "What do you take me for? I wouldn't let him into the house. We walked and talked. He started by apologizing, which was nice."

"Don't fall for it, Anna." Sammy's voice held more than a trace of warning.

"I know, I know. I didn't, believe me. Like I said, he *started* by apologizing but then later tried to act like everything was back to normal between us. He even tried to defend his actions for stealing my research."

Sammy let out an annoyed breath. "That man. And bad timing, too, huh, with everything else going on?"

"So that's the other thing. It wasn't a coincidence. He said he came down because he'd read about Oliver's death in the paper, knew him, and wanted to see if he could help. 'To pay his respects,' he said."

"That's the dumbest thing I've ever heard." Sammy snorted in derision. "How could he help? And pay his respects where, at the morgue?"

"I know, right?" Anna leaned forward to put her empty cereal bowl on the coffee table in front of her and turned to look out the bay window. She rubbed a hand over Tough Cookie's back. It was dark outside, but the streetlamps cast orbs of yellow light against the windowpanes, and she could just make out the shapes of the porch furniture. "I have to wonder, Sammy, if he had an ulterior motive."

"Like trying to get you back, you mean?" Sammy asked.

"Yeesss..." Anna stretched out the word. "Like that, or..."

On the other end of the line, a chair scraped against the floor. "You think he killed the guy! You think Steve killed Oliver?"

Anna laughed at Sammy's enthusiasm. "I wouldn't put it past him, but that's crazy. Isn't it? I mean, Steve's a jerk, not a murderer."

"Well, he must have said something or done something to make you even think that. What was it?"

"Partly, it's just the timing. It's quite a coincidence, you know? And his explanation really doesn't make sense. He says he just came to town this morning, but how can I trust him? I know he lies. He might be lying about that. He's skipping the annual conference, and it's in Philly this year."

"Hm, that sounds like a good reason to get out of town to me. Annual conference?" Sammy asked.

"It's actually a big deal. We used to look forward to it every year. It's a chance to reconnect with colleagues, share notes, you know."

"Steve might not want to run into any old colleagues right now," Sammy pointed out.

"Yeah, that's true. I asked him about that, and he denied it, of course." She pictured him standing on the front porch when she'd first opened the door, the sad look in his eyes, the way he'd apologized instead of getting angry, like he used to. "I miss him," she said softly, leaning forward to hold Tough Cookie closer, feeling the cat purr against her chest.

"Oh, honey. I know. But remember, it's not him you miss. You miss the person you thought he was."

Anna nodded. Of course Sammy was right. She knew that. At least, her brain knew that. She wasn't sure what her heart knew right then, but she could admit to herself that when she'd seen Steve that morning, she'd felt a frisson of excitement, a tang of attraction. And that really annoyed her.

"Anna, you still there?" Sammy's voice shook Anna out of her reverie.

"I'm here. And I'm definitely adding Steve to my suspect list. Maybe I'm just still angry at him, but it's weird that he's here now."

"Okay, so he was in town, and he knew the victim. How about motive and means? Do you know any more about how Oliver died?"

Anna tickled Tough Cookie behind the ears as she

related to Sammy all that Evan had told her earlier, leaving out the more disturbing details.

"Right. So... is Steve big enough to have strangled an average-size man?" Sammy asked.

Anna pictured his strong arms wrapped around her, his hands on her face when he bent to kiss her. "He is." Her voice caught. She coughed to clear her throat. "Yep, definitely."

"All right. How about access to the water?"

"Well, anyone could walk down by the creek, I guess," Anna said. Though, picturing the creek, that was highly unlikely. No paths lined the bank, so anyone who wanted to walk there would have to fight through swampy grasslands. "But that's probably not what happened. More likely, whoever killed Oliver pushed him off a boat, and Steve doesn't have a boat."

"He could have rented one, though. Right?" Sammy pointed out.

"Of course. That's it." Anna leaned forward in her excitement. "We can find out if Steve rented a boat for his time here, and I can try talking to some of the people he mentioned. Maybe they know something about what he's really doing down here or about his relationship with the victim."

Sammy laughed. "Yes we can. Wow, you really want to prove Steve did this. Don't you?"

Anna shrugged into the phone. "Maybe, maybe not. But I don't mind the idea of getting him into a little hot water."

❧ 14 ☙

Anna trotted back into the kitchen from the summer dining room to refill one of her dainty porcelain pitchers with cream. The sun shone brightly that morning, the weather prediction warm enough to justify serving breakfast on the wide porch. Anna had followed Great-Aunt Louise's plan, using the small room at the front of the house that might tradition-ally have been called a morning room, with French doors opening up onto the porch, as a summer dining room. Though she set up two tables indoors, in case any guests preferred not to eat alfresco, all the guests had opted for the tables set out on the porch, looking out over the garden.

Eoin finished his breakfast in the kitchen then skipped outside to chat with—and charm—the guests.

Tough Cookie, unusually, opted to stay indoors. She perched on a padded window seat next to the French doors, watching Anna flit back and forth between her guests and the kitchen, occasionally licking a paw and cleaning behind her ears.

"Am I boring you?" Anna asked the cat as she returned from carrying the cream to the porch along with a bowl of freshly cut strawberries. "I'm sorry my conversation isn't more scintillating."

She was using each pass-through to explain to the cat that she decided to do a little research on Steve and the people he had mentioned. As she whisked up another batch of scrambled eggs and slid more bread into the toaster, she scanned the various web pages she'd pulled up on her laptop sitting open on the counter next to her. Preparing and serving breakfast required energy and enthusiasm but not concentration. While her hands were busy mixing, her mind was on other matters.

A quick web search didn't uncover whether Steve had hired a boat in Cape May. She wasn't too surprised by that. Now who were the other people Steve had mentioned? She thought for a moment then snapped her fingers. Brad Atherton.

A series of web pages popped up in a list. This looked promising, too. She started clicking.

The toast popping brought her attention back to her food, and she realized the eggs were very nearly over-cooked. She plated the new meal, grabbed a basket of muffins, and headed back to the dining room.

"Nothing but details about his research so far," she told Tough Cookie as she passed. "Some citations in articles, references to him on linguistic web sites, that sort of thing."

Tough Cookie blinked in response.

As always, Anna took her time as she served her guests, asking them about their activities the day before and their plans for the day. Cape May had such a variety of options for visitors. She liked to make sure the guests of Climbing Rose Cottage had all the information they needed to plan a perfect vacation. Eoin continued mingling with the guests, who cooed over his bright-red hair and lilting Irish accent.

"Aren't you a darling!" One older woman ruffled Eoin's hair as she complimented him. "What did you say your name was, Owen?"

"Eoin." Eoin explained patiently.

"Oween?" the woman tried again.

Eoin shook his head but bit his tongue.

"How do you know so much about this town?" she continued.

"By reading, of course." Eoin grinned and leaned into the arm of her chair. "I love to read. And I'll be here all summer, so there's lots of time to learn more. Now, what else d'you want to know about our town?"

An animated discussion about the bird sanctuary near the lighthouse took Anna's mind off murder, and as she returned to the kitchen, her thoughts were on egrets and swans. Tough Cookie's meow brought her mind back to Climbing Rose Cottage and the research she'd been doing on Brad Atherton.

"Right, thanks. I should see what I can find out about the person, not just the linguist."

She rinsed another basket of strawberries, patting them dry with a dishtowel before trimming and slicing them. She tried again with a new set of search terms, this time looking for information about Brad's family. She scrolled through two screens of unrelated information before she noticed an old newspaper clipping from a town in Maine. Curious, she clicked it open.

The story only mentioned Brad in passing, as one of several children of a local political figure. The article itself focused on Mrs. Atherton, Brad's mother, apparently an important society figure in that area.

Anna frowned as she considered whether this information was helpful or not. "What do you think?" she asked Tough Cookie, passing by with another bowl of strawberries. "He's the son of a prominent couple, definitely rich, blue blood, that sort of thing. Could he be the type of person who would talk to me about Steve? Or Oliver?"

Tough Cookie meowed. Anna considered the response carefully then continued to the porch. She was getting pretty good at multitasking. Taking it to a whole new level, in fact. On the other hand, she might be driving herself crazy in the process. She was, after all, talking to a cat. She refused to address Tough Cookie on her way back to the kitchen.

She was definitely getting somewhere. If only she could figure out where. She let out a breath and reached over to close her laptop. As she leaned toward it, she noticed the link at the bottom of the newspaper article. It was a link to the Cape May Marina, where Mr. Atherton kept his boat.

Anna's excitement rose as she followed the link. The boat was still there, docked in Cape May, and the current owner was listed as Brad Atherton. Now that was interesting.

She grabbed another serving bowl and ran it out to the guests, then stopped in front of Tough Cookie on her way back from the porch to get a second opinion. "Am I crazy to even consider contacting him without calling the police?" she asked the cat. "Brad doesn't know me, so he has no reason to talk to me. What if there's no connection at all between his boat and the murder?"

Tough Cookie blinked, licked her paw, and rubbed behind her ear.

"Right." Anna nodded once. "You're right. I need to learn more."

Back in the kitchen, she typed in the other name Steve had mentioned, Tara Blanche.

She wasn't familiar with the name, but Steve had implied she should have recognized it. It didn't take much effort to find the website of Tara Blanche, internationally renowned writer of speculative fiction, poetry, and literary fiction.

"Wow." Anna scrolled through the list of awards the writer had won, the collection of recognitions. "Impressive." Anna was a little embarrassed she hadn't heard of her before. Clearly, she was reading the wrong things.

She reached the bottom of the page and quickly scrolled back up. As she did, she looked more closely at the pictures at the top of the site. Did that face look familiar? She leaned closer, narrowing her eyes. There was no mistaking it. She was staring at a photograph of her single guest, Donna White.

15

By ten o'clock, Anna had cleared the tables on the porch and thoroughly cleaned the kitchen, double-checking to make sure she had the ingredients for the cookies she would bake that afternoon. Most of her guests were off enjoying themselves, as well they should be. All except Donna White, aka Tara Blanch.

Anna hadn't accosted Tara at breakfast—she still had some professional pride. But maybe the writer would have a minute to talk to her now. She set up a tray with tea and a few biscuits, ran upstairs, and tapped lightly on Tara's door.

"Hello? Ms. Blanch?" she called when her knock received no response.

She jumped back when the door sprang open.

Tara looked even more annoyed than usual. "So, you know my real name. I wish you didn't. Please don't tell anyone."

"Oh. Right. Sorry. I thought you might like some tea?" Anna gestured with the tray.

"Hm. Fine. Now go away." Tara took the tray roughly from Anna and moved to close the door.

"Wait." Anna put out a hand to hold the door open.

Tara glared at her.

"I'm sorry. I was hoping... that is, I wanted to ask you about Oliver Humphreys-Gibbons. I understand you were friends."

Tara glared for a second more. "I'm here to work. I travel under a false name so that people won't know it's me and won't bother me. How many times do I have to say this? Go away and leave me alone." She kicked the door, and it slammed shut.

Well! Anna's hands balled into fists, and she took a few deep breaths. Of course, what Tara said made sense. She was a famous writer. If she came to Cape May for privacy, then it might make sense to use a fake name. Anna wouldn't be a good host if she kept bugging her. But just because she didn't want to harass her guest didn't mean she would give up. She ran back downstairs, called for Eoin, and headed out into the glorious day. At least she knew Felicia would be willing to talk with her.

Felicia's home sat in a row of similarly detailed Victorian houses, each with their individual interpretations of gables, towers, turrets, decorative gingerbread trims, and wide porches that defined the architectural style. Felicia's house was painted a pale blue that almost glowed against the dark-blue trim. All the windows on the ground floor stood open, and sheer curtains fluttered behind the screens.

"Hello?" Anna called out cheerfully as she knocked on the front door.

She heard footsteps approaching before the door flung open. "Anna, Eoin, what a surprise. Come in. Felicia is back in the kitchen."

Anna greeted Felicia's partner, Kathy, with a quick hug and followed her toward the back of the house. While the outside of the house might look like it belonged in the nineteenth century, the kitchen had been completely modernized. Yet it somehow managed to keep its historic feel, with a wood burner in the corner and dark walnut cabinetry.

"Anna, Eoin, good to see you both. I'm just heading out, I'm afraid." Felicia greeted them as she finished a cup of coffee and placed the mug in the dishwasher.

"I know. I'm glad I caught you. I wanted to talk with you—with both of you." She looked at Kathy. "I'm trying to find some information that only a local would know."

"Shoot," Kathy said. "What can I tell you about dear Cape May?"

"Well... it's about her residents, actually. I have two questions. First, I'm trying to find some information about a man who keeps a boat at the Cape May Marina."

Felicia grinned at Kathy, who raised her eyebrows and shrugged. "I row, Anna. That doesn't mean I know everything about boats and who has them."

"I know." Anna laughed. "But you two know so much about this town and the people in it." She tilted her head. "And how to find out more."

Kathy let out a breath and shook her head. "Gossip again, is it?" She pulled out a chair from the kitchen table and sat, her legs spread wide, her arms folded across her chest.

"Sorry." Anna slid into a chair across the table. "I know you don't like to gossip. But I just found out that a friend—well, a colleague, anyway—of the man who was killed keeps a boat at the Cape May Marina. His name is Brad Atherton."

Kathy narrowed her eyes. "And this interests you, why?"

"I'm sorry. I should have told you." Felicia moved to stand behind Kathy, one hand on her shoulder. "The police seem to suspect Lorenzo Cortinas in this murder, and Brooke asked Anna to help prove he wasn't involved."

Kathy threw her head back and laughed. "To help the police? That's ridiculous."

Anna felt her face grow red. "Well, maybe not to help the police. But it doesn't hurt, does it? And if it makes Brooke feel better to know that someone's out there asking questions that don't implicate her uncle in murder...?"

Kathy still smiled as she shook her head. "I get it. It must be hard for Brooke, with her parents just moving away two years ago and now questions about her uncle."

"And that's my other question." Anna grimaced apologetically. "I'm trying to figure out why the police would want to question Lorenzo. Why do they think he might be involved?"

Felicia frowned. "Wouldn't the best person to answer that question be Lorenzo himself? How would we know?"

Anna looked down at her hands, folded on the table in front of her. "I'm sorry, I know I'm basically asking you to gossip."

"About a neighbor and a friend," Kathy pointed out.

"Right. Okay, forget I asked. I'll talk to Lorenzo directly."

"Good call," Kathy said.

Felicia patted Kathy's shoulder then moved out to the hall. "I'm sorry, ladies, but I really must go." She grabbed the satchel that sat on a bench in the hall. "Will you walk with me, Anna?"

"Of course." Anna jumped up, glad to get away from Kathy's intimidating stare.

"Anna." Kathy's voice was surprisingly gentle, and Anna turned to her. "I'll see what I can find out about the Atherton person, okay?"

"Thank you," Anna responded gratefully. "I know I'm

not the police, but Brooke did ask for my help. And..." Anna paused, not ready to share her feelings about her ex-boyfriend with Kathy just yet. "Other people must know more about Oliver Humphreys-Gibbons."

"Of course." Kathy nodded. "Detective Walsh, for one. It's his job, after all. And"—Kathy took a sip of her coffee —"if anyone with a boat at Cape May Marina is involved, Detective Walsh would know. He keeps his own boat at Bluff Point Boatyard, just along the bay from the Cape May Marina."

Anna blinked, surprised. "Detective Walsh has a boat?"

Kathy's brow lowered in confusion. "Sure. Why not?"

"Anna, are you coming?" Felicia called from the hall.

"Right, yes. Coming!" Anna called. "Thank you so much, Kathy. Anything you can find I would really appreciate." She trotted toward the front door and her waiting friend and cousin.

✤ 16 ✤

"Now, tell me." Felicia tucked Anna's arm under hers. "Why are you asking about this Brad fellow? We'll be at the library in ten minutes, so you better start talking."

Anna watched Eoin running ahead of them, jumping to swing at the branches that hung low over the sidewalk. She pulled her arm free and reached out to push a low-hanging tree branch out of the way, tearing off a leaf as she did so. "My ex-boyfriend is in town, Steve."

"Ah." Felicia's tone clearly indicated she remembered the situation that had driven Anna from her research.

"Anyway, Steve knew Oliver, the victim, and he mentioned a bunch of other people who knew him too."

"Including Brad Atherton."

Anna nodded. "He's just one of the people Steve mentioned—a guy who worked closely with Oliver. I figured if I was going to ask questions about Oliver, I should start with someone who knew him well. I tried talking to one of my guests—she was friends with Oliver, and she's traveling under an assumed name, which is clearly suspicious—but she said she's working and doesn't have time to talk. Then, when I found out Brad had a boat down here..." She shrugged as she tore at the leaf.

"You have a guest traveling under an assumed name?" Felicia asked. "Isn't that a lot more suspicious than someone who happens to have a boat at Cape May Marina?"

"I know, but her explanation makes sense. She's a famous author and said she likes to travel incognito."

Felicia raised her eyebrows. "What author?"

Anna lowered her voice. "I shouldn't tell you. I'm probably breaking some kind of B and B owner code, but it's Tara Blanch."

"Really?" Felicia sounded impressed. "She's an inspiring writer. I've read everything she's written. All right then, I can see why you're focusing on Brad Atherton instead. But remember, just because the man knew the victim doesn't mean he was involved."

"No, no, of course not," Anna answered quickly. "It's just a place to start." She narrowed her eyes as she spoke. "I really want to know Steve's true reason for being down here. I was kind of hoping Brad might have some ideas about that. Steve talked like he knows Brad well."

Felicia rolled her eyes. "You want Steve to be the killer. Is that it?"

Anna grinned. "Maybe. But no." She shook her head firmly. "I know he's not. I know the man. He may be a liar and a cheat, but he's no killer." She held up a finger. "He is arrogant enough that he could be manipulated fairly easily, though. What if someone else tricked him into coming down here?"

"Someone with a nefarious plan, you mean?" Felicia laughed. "I suspect you're making this way more complicated than you need to. A man was killed. That means someone hated him enough to kill him. You need to find the person who really hated him."

"True." Anna nodded, thinking. "But that person also has to have means and opportunity, right? And in this case, that means access to the creek, probably on a boat. And the chance to be alone with Oliver to..." Anna shut her eyes. "To strangle him to death and push him overboard."

She felt Felicia shudder beside her. "That is quite horrible."

"I know. The police must think Lorenzo has motive. I don't know what it is. But Steve is in the wrong place at the wrong time, and that's weird, right? Then this guy Brad isn't involved, but it turns out he has a boat down here. That's weird, too, right?"

"Right..." Felicia stretched out the word. "And then there's Luke, who had an argument with the man just before he was killed."

It was Anna's turn to roll her eyes. "But we both know Luke wasn't involved."

"Okay, okay. So, who else knew the victim and had reason to hate him?"

Anna shrugged again. "That's what I need to find out. That's why I want to talk to this guy, Brad. He knew the victim. He knows the town, since he keeps his boat here. Maybe he can point me in a different direction. Tara Blanch clearly won't help."

"Ms. Keane." The high-pitched voice carried ahead of the girl who trotted up to them. "I thought that was you. Ms. McGregor, nice to see you again."

Eoin squeaked and ran to BethAnne, sliding his hand into hers and looking up at her, his face awash in admiration. The girl, almost old enough to be considered a young woman, grinned widely, her white teeth practically glowing in the sunlight.

Wasn't he too young for a crush, Anna wondered as she greeted the girl. "Nice to see you, too, BethAnne. What're you so happy about?"

BethAnne laughed as she shrugged. "I have the whole afternoon free. I finished my chores early, and my mom said I could do whatever I wanted."

"And of course you want to go to the library." Anna shook her head incredulously.

"Yep." BethAnne nodded, the beads at the ends of her many braids bouncing against one another. "You got it. What're you guys talking about? Did I hear you mention Tara Blanch?"

"Oh, uh," Felicia muttered, obviously unwilling to talk to this child about murder.

"I did." Anna jumped in to relieve her friend. "She's staying at Climbing Rose Cottage. Do you know her?"

"Know her? Hardly." BethAnne snorted a laugh. "I know about her, though. She's a world-famous writer. That's so cool that she's staying at your B and B. Is she awesome?"

"Um, sure. Yeah." Anna didn't have the heart to burst BethAnne's dreams. "I'm also looking for a friend—well, a friend of a friend. He's a professor of linguistics at my old university."

"Ooh." BethAnne's eyes lit up. "A professor of linguistics. That field is so cool—the scientific study of language." BethAnne paused for only a second. "Did you know that linguists, I mean real linguists, have to understand fields like neuroscience, psychology, anthropology, computer science... they're totally multidisciplinary."

"Yes, I knew that." Anna grinned as she looked at Felicia over BethAnne's head.

They had continued their trek to the library, and she could see it now, just a block ahead.

"How do you know so much about linguistics, BethAnne?"

The look BethAnne gave Anna made it very clear she'd asked a stupid question.

"Right, sorry." Anna held up a hand. "Debate team."

"Yep," BethAnne nodded gaily. "When I studied it, I wanted to learn more about phonetics, but we focused on the whole field instead."

"Phonetics?" Felicia asked.

"The study of the sounds of speech," Anna answered. "How we—humans, that is—produce sounds, how we hear sounds. It's pretty cool."

BethAnne glanced at Anna out of the corner of her eye. "Do you know about electropalatography?"

Anna was impressed that the young woman only stumbled over the word once. "I do, but you tell me. What do you like about it?"

"It's just cool." BethAnne shrugged. She turned to Felicia. "They use this electric tool that they shape to fit someone's mouth, then it records how that person's tongue moves as they speak. Neat, huh?"

"Uh-huh." Felicia's eyes opened wide, and she looked at Anna again. "Neat. But I'm surprised you're so interested in it, BethAnne. I always thought you were more interested in politics."

They reached the library, and BethAnne happily followed Felicia up the path to the front door.

"I'm going to leave you two here," Anna interrupted. "I need to... do some research of my own. Coming, Eoin?"

Eoin, who had contentedly trotted along, silently holding BethAnne's hand, looked back at her. "Can't I stay here, Cousin Anna? With BethAnne?" He looked up at BethAnne, and Anna could've sworn he batted his eyelashes.

"It's okay with me, but only if BethAnne and Felicia agree. They'll be responsible for you."

"Please? Please?" Eoin turned his big eyes to Felicia, who found them impossible to resist.

"Sure, okay." Felicia nodded at Anna. "Now you be careful, all right? Don't start offending people with your questions. Again." She raised an eyebrow to emphasize the last word.

Anna grinned, waved, and turned to go. As she left, she heard BethAnne's young voice.

"I do like politics, Ms. Keane. I wouldn't want to be a linguist, but I love learning about linguistics. And the more I know, the better I'll be at politics, right?"

Anna shook her head as she walked. That girl really was a genius. It was going to get her into trouble one day.

For her part, Anna still needed answers to her questions. What information could she find about Brad Atherton and about why the police suspected Lorenzo? She needed a local's insight, and she knew one other local she could count on.

17

The bike ride to Luke's house in West Cape May took less than ten minutes. At least it would have if Anna hadn't taken the longer route, following Beach Avenue for the first few minutes and pausing to appreciate the beauty of her new hometown. On a day as perfect as this one, she didn't feel guilty. She used the extra time to compose her thoughts, focusing on the questions she wanted to ask Luke but also letting her mind work its way around what she knew, in case she came up with other questions she hadn't thought of yet.

Luke lived in a rancher a block off Sunset Boulevard. It was an old house but well-kept. The expansive yard that surrounded the property told another story, however. Luke was clearly a builder, not a gardener. Patches of dirt fought the weedy grass for space. Flower beds overflowed with reeds and hogweed instead of flowers.

The house itself looked spectacular. Anna knew that Luke had purchased it not long after taking on his business. Abandoned and ignored, the old property had been on the market for years, but no one had been willing to attempt the renovations required to bring it up to living standards, no one except Luke. Luke saw the house as a challenge, like an old painting that simply needed a little restoration and care—actually, a lot of restoration and care.

He'd done an impressive job, Anna thought as she approached the house across the disastrous front yard. The white paint on the new wooden shingles reflected the bright morning sun. Dark-blue shutters lined wide windows, and Anna could see that these weren't simply decorative shutters—with hinges and locks, they could be propped open, as they were now, or pulled closed to keep out the harsh summer sun. Luke had added a covered porch wide enough to hold a small table and two chairs, a perfect place to sit and look out over the marshlands that separated West Cape May from the ocean.

Following the faint music that carried from the back of the house, Anna took the path leading around the side toward the separate garage. "Hello? Luke?" she called as she walked, not wanting to surprise him.

Turning the corner at the back of the house, the first thing Anna noticed was the boat. Well, to be fair, she first noticed Luke standing with his back to her as he applied a coat of some kind of varnish to the outside of the boat, his back muscles shifting as he brushed back and forth. But the important thing, Anna realized, was the boat.

"Luke!" Anna called again.

Luke heard her that time. He turned and grinned. "Hey, Anna, what brings you out here?" He brushed a clump of hair from his forehead, using the back of his wrist to wipe the sweat from his brow.

He'd ignored the backyard as steadily as he had the front. Luke had less property back there, as his land ended where his neighbor's began, but what he had he had turned into an outdoor workstation. Covered shelves lined the wall of the garage, facing a concrete pad that took up half his backyard. The boat stood on that pad on a trailer that could be attached to his truck.

"Luke, I didn't know you had a boat."

"Oh yeah." He turned to look at the boat. "She's small, but she's powerful. I got her super cheap because of her condition. But it didn't take too much work to fix her up. What do you think?"

Anna walked around the boat, admiring it. "It's beautiful."

Luke had applied his carpentry skills to an old wooden fishing boat, the kind that tended to show up as wrecks along the beach more often than staying afloat. But under Luke's skilled hands, the craft seemed ready to take on the ocean's waves. Pale-blue paint covered the outside and the console, which looked like two boxes attached to each other. On the inside, however, Luke had sanded and varnished the wood into a golden glow, with low benches that ran along the sides of the boat from front to back—or bow to stern.

"I've been working on her for about a year now." Luke ran a proud hand along the side. "She's almost ready, still in time for the summer flounder season." He took a deep breath as he admired his handiwork a little more then turned back to Anna. "So, what's up? What can I do for you?" He frowned. "Did something break? Is it an emergency?" He walked toward her. "You could've just called."

"No, no." Anna waved her hands. "Nothing's wrong. The house is great. I just wanted..." she chewed her lip. "It's such a gorgeous day. I wanted to go for a bike ride. And I've never seen your house, so I figured..."

Luke raised one eyebrow. "Come on in then. Lemonade?"

Anna followed Luke inside, passing through a living

room that spanned the length of the house. At the far end of the room, a red-brick surround showed off a fireplace that looked big enough to stand in, while tall windows lined one wall. From that room, they passed through a smaller dining room into a kitchen with a cozy eating area set up next to one of the big front windows. Anna already knew Luke had the instincts of an interior designer, so the allure of the place didn't surprise her. The freshly squeezed lemonade and homemade cookies did, however.

"Did you bake these?" she asked, her voice muffled as she chewed.

"I did." Luke grinned, taking a bite of his own. "I guess I'm just full of surprises. Now, what can I do for you? Really, I mean."

Anna coughed, choking on her cookie, and took a sip of her lemonade. "Right. Well, I have a couple of questions about the town that I thought you could help me with."

Luke leaned back in his chair and crossed his arms over his chest. "Shoot."

"Okay." Anna leaned back as well. "Have you ever heard of Brad Atherton? He doesn't live locally—he's from up near Philly—but he keeps a boat in the Cape May Marina."

Luke frowned. "Atherton. You know, I think I've heard that name. I don't spend a lot of time at that marina. It's a little out of my price range." He grinned ruefully. "But yeah, I think I've heard the name."

"Anything interesting?" Anna leaned forward on the table.

Luke shook his head. "No, just the name rings a bell. Why do you need to know? Want me to ask around?"

"Hm. Maybe." Anna considered his offer. "Yeah, okay. I'm trying to get in touch with him. He worked with Oliver, you see. I figured he might know something that would explain—"

"Wait. Oliver the dead guy?" Luke cut her off.

Anna nodded. "I told Brooke I would try to help her out. The police seem to think her uncle, Lorenzo, is somehow involved, but that doesn't make sense."

"Oh no?" Luke laughed. "It makes a lot of sense to me."

"Why?"

"Lorenzo? That man's involved in way too many scams to be innocent. He's always up to something. I heard that before he moved to Cape May, he worked the festival circuit, ripping people off left and right."

"Festival circuit?"

"Sure, you know. Traveling festivals that move from town to town. Lorenzo's a magician, so it's the perfect setup for him."

Anna frowned and took another cookie. "Hm. Well, that was my second question."

Luke leaned forward, resting his forearms on the table. "Anna, you shouldn't get involved in this. You know that."

Anna shrugged and nibbled her cookie.

Luke rested a hand on her arm. "Anna, do you hear me? I don't want you to put yourself in danger again."

Anna lingered for a minute, enjoying the feel of his hand on her arm, then pulled back. "I won't. I promise. I just want to make Brooke feel better, let her know that the police are looking at other suspects too."

Luke leaned back in his chair. "Are they?"

"If they aren't, they should."

"Why do I think you have someone particular in mind, and it's not Brad Atherton?"

Anna looked at the table and shrugged. "Don't you think it's weird that Steve showed up in town just after Oliver was killed?"

"Your ex? Yeah, it's definitely weird, but he explained that it's not a coincidence. I mean, he's not trying to hide the fact that he knew Oliver or that he's interested in the murder."

"I guess. But what if something else is going on? And what if Brad knows more about Steve's actions than we do? Steve seemed to really admire Brad, like he looks up to him. Maybe Brad has some insight."

Luke shut his eyes and shook his head. "So you want to get involved in this investigation to prove that your ex is a murderer? That's nuts, Anna."

"No, no." Anna tossed her napkin on the table. "That does sound nuts when you say it out loud. I don't really think he's a killer. I just... I don't know."

"Maybe you need to prove to yourself that he's not? You already feel bad enough about your relationship with him. I bet you'd feel even worse if he turned out to be a killer as well as a liar and a cheat."

Anna looked at him from under her hair. "How did you get so smart?"

Luke sighed. "All right. I'll see what I can find out about our friend Brad. But don't get your hopes too high, Anna. Like I said, Lorenzo's a character. The cops may have good reason to think he's involved."

18

Anna meandered along Washington Street, peering into the stores she passed without really seeing the goods displayed in their windows. Neither did she pay much attention to the crowd of beachgoers strolling along with her, chatting, laughing, yelling. Her mind was on Brooke and what Luke had told her about Lorenzo.

All afternoon, as she'd finished cleaning the rooms and prepared tea for her guests, she had turned this new information over in her mind. Lorenzo had a reputation as a crook. How much credibility could she attribute to this rumor, though? Just because Luke heard it didn't make it true. Perhaps that was why Kathy was always so reluctant to participate in the gossip channel. Half of what got passed on was false, the other half greatly exaggerated. But every now and then, Anna knew, she gleaned a kernel of truth.

"Hey, you." Sammy waved, struggling to get Anna's attention.

Anna blinked and shook herself out of her reverie

enough to wave back as her friend approached. "Hi, Sammy." They hugged a greeting. "Thanks for meeting me here."

Sammy looked up and down the street. "No problem. Do you have a new restaurant you want to check out?"

"Hmmm, not exactly." Anna had arranged to meet Sammy for an early dinner but figured she could address at least one of her concerns in the process.

Sammy's eyes narrowed. "You're up to something. What is it? And can I be part of it?" She grinned as she finished.

"You sure can. Come on." Anna grabbed Sammy's hand and led her toward the Magic Shop. "First, you really do need to see Brooke's shop. But also, I need to talk to Brooke. Luke told me some things about Lorenzo that got me thinking."

"Uh-oh, what kind of things?"

"Just come on." Anna picked up her pace, leading the way until the street dead-ended at Perry Street.

Brooke and Lorenzo's Magic Shop stood on the corner, an inconspicuous sign over the door reading simply "Magic Shop." Across the street, groups of people gathered around tables outside the coffee shop, but Anna's side of the street remained quiet.

Anna pulled open the door, and Sammy followed her in. The air inside was cool, and the gentle tinkle of a water fountain came from somewhere in the back. Various scents of herbs and incense assaulted her nose, but after only a moment, she adapted to it and found the smell oddly calming.

"Wow. You weren't kidding." Sammy's eyes opened wide as she made her way along one aisle of the small store, peering closely at items as she passed. "It's like Dungeons and Dragons meets Harry Potter meets Merlin meets..."

Her voice trailed off as she apparently ran out of famous characters to compare to the store.

"I know. It's great. Isn't it?" Brooke entered from a back room. "I'm so glad you're here, Anna. And, Sammy, you haven't been to the store before. Have you?"

Anna greeted her friend and waited as Brooke gave Sammy the grand tour. It didn't take too long, as the store only had four short aisles. An awful lot of merchandise was packed into the small space, however.

"Brooke, I was hoping to talk with Lorenzo. Is he here?" Anna asked once the tour ended.

Brooke nodded then yelled, "Uncle!" at the top of her voice. "Sorry," she said at a normal decibel. "He's a little deaf."

Lorenzo shuffled in from the back room, his attention focused on the book he held in his hands. "Yes, yes, what is it? You don't need to shout." Lorenzo, a bear of a man, had curly black hair that touched his neck in the back and hung over his forehead. More black chest hair peeked out above his button-down shirt. The sparkle in his eyes belied the complaining nature of his words, and when he reached the group of women, he leaned over and kissed the top of Brooke's head. "What can I do for you, darling?"

He glanced at Anna and Sammy as if just noticing them for the first time. "Can I help you?"

"Mr. Cortinas." Anna put out a hand. "I'm Anna McGregor, and this is Sammy Shields. We're friends of Brooke."

"Pleasure to meet you. And please, call me Lorenzo." He said the name with a bit of a trill, and Anna caught the shadow of a gesture as he said it, a movement reminiscent of his magical performances.

"Lorenzo." Anna nodded. "I'm not sure if Brooke told you..." Her words dropped off as Brooke shook her head frantically behind her uncle. "Um... I'm not sure if Brooke told you that I'm interested in learning more about Cape May." She finished her sentence, and Brooke let out an audible breath.

Lorenzo glanced at his niece then turned back to Anna. "I'm sorry, but I've only lived here a couple of years. Surely Brooke is the person you want to talk to. She grew up here, after all."

"Right, right. And I did talk to her. But you see..." Anna fumbled for words.

"Part of what makes Cape May so charming is the way people flock here from all over the world," Sammy jumped in.

"Right, exactly," Anna said, relieved. "You. The Ahavas."

"So it would be fun to know why you came to Cape May and what you were doing before that?" Sammy finished the question.

Lorenzo listened to their explanation, but his eyes remained fixed on his niece, narrowing with every word Anna and Sammy said. "Brooke, is this true?"

Brooke swallowed, looked hopefully from Anna to Sammy, then back to her uncle. She shook her head. "No, Uncle. I'm sorry. I put them up to this."

"M-hm," he replied.

Now it was Anna's turn to blush. "I'm so sorry, Lorenzo. I didn't want to lie to you."

"No, no." Lorenzo waved the apology away with a hand. "I understand how Brooke works. Believe me. Fortunately, you can't con a con, can you?" He grinned.

"Actually, that's what I wanted to ask you about," Anna said.

Sammy shook her head and turned away, but Anna heard her mumble, "Oh my goodness."

"I beg your pardon?" Lorenzo stood a little taller.

"Uncle, I asked Anna to help figure out why the police might think you were involved in that man's murder."

Lorenzo's face turned red, and his cheeks puffed out. Anna took a step back until she felt a shelf against her back. Lorenzo looked like he was about to explode. Anna glanced at Sammy, who looked as nervous as she felt.

"Uncle?" Brooke asked tentatively, reaching out to touch him then pulling back.

Finally, Lorenzo let out his breath and shook his head. Anna blew out the breath she'd been holding and slumped against the shelf.

"Why didn't you just ask me?" Lorenzo asked in a quiet voice.

"I did. I tried to when the police were here this morning, but you wouldn't answer me."

"Of course I wouldn't answer you in front of them. Never trust the police. I'm sure I've told you that."

Brooke shook her head. "No, I'm pretty sure I'd remember that."

"Why don't you trust the police, Lorenzo?" Anna asked.

Lorenzo shuffled over to the tall stool behind the register and leaned against it. The three women gathered around him, waiting for his story.

"I imagine Brooke already told you that I came here two years ago to open this shop."

Anna and Sammy nodded, so Lorenzo continued.

"Before that, I did a lot of things. I worked where I could find employment. I'm a very good magician. Did you know?"

Anna nodded, even though she had no real idea.

"Oh, yes," the old man continued. "I worked at Cooney Island, Ocean City, even Las Vegas."

"I heard you worked the festival route," Anna chimed in uncertainly.

Lorenzo lifted one eyebrow and smiled. "You heard that, did you? I guess gossip really does spread in a small town. Yes, I did. I loved it. I love magic. I love thrilling people. But I also need to make a living. You understand?"

The women nodded again.

Lorenzo took another deep breath. "Two years ago, before joining Brooke here, in Cape May, I was part of a group that sold miracle cures for a number of ailments."

"Ailments?" Sammy frowned.

Lorenzo raised an eyebrow. "Indeed. One of those ailments was a lisp. We sold an essential oil that you put on your tongue, just a few drops, every day. We would explain to our customers that the cure wasn't immediate, but eventually, the lisp would go away. And of course, we would advise them to continue with their regular speech therapy as well. We weren't hurting anyone."

Anna frowned. "You sold them something they believed would help. But it didn't really help, did it?"

Lorenzo shrugged. "Natural remedies are tricky, my dear. They don't work like modern medicine, but they can be very powerful indeed."

"Hmm." Anna bit her tongue before she said anything rude. She had a lot of respect for natural remedies. She'd focused her research on indigenous remedies, after all, tracing the migration of such remedies from Puebla to Philadelphia, how they were used in each, how understandings of medicine varied and were incorporated into people's lives. But her interest was from a purely scientific standpoint. She suspected Lorenzo wasn't quite as concerned as she was with the science.

"This man heard about us. He was a linguist, involved in some sort of speech therapy. He heard what we were doing and contacted the police. He claimed we were practicing medicine without a license, practicing fraudulently."

"And were you?" Anna asked.

"Eh. Maybe." Lorenzo shrugged. "But I've moved on now. I love it here in Cape May. Opening this store, spending time with my niece, getting out on my boat. What more could I ask for in life?"

"And this man, this linguist," Anna said. "Was he Oliver Humphreys-Gibbons?"

Lorenzo nodded. "He was, and now he's dead."

19

Brooke walked Sammy and Anna out of the store, apologizing as they went. "I had no idea, Anna. He never told me... how could I know he knew the dead guy?"

"You couldn't, Brooke. It's okay." Anna did her best to comfort her friend. "But it sounds like the police have very good reason to suspect Lorenzo."

Brooke wiped a tear from her eye, and her lips trembled. "But he didn't do it. I know he didn't. He couldn't have."

Sammy put an arm around Brooke's shoulders. "We know, honey. We're still here for you. Just because a man has a complicated past doesn't make him a criminal in the present."

Anna smiled gratefully at Sammy for expressing that so well. She was about to join in the sentiment when a squeal of tires followed by a shout drew her attention to a red sports car pulling up along the road. The car must have done an illegal U-turn in the middle of the road, based on the skid marks left on the pavement. The shout presumably came from a man who looked like he'd just leapt out of the way of the careening vehicle.

"What are you doing, you madman?" the man shouted again.

No one in the car moved, so the man gave up with a frustrated wave of his hand, turning to continue his walk along the pedestrianized street.

Once the angry pedestrian had moved away, the passenger door popped open. An Asian man in his mid-twenties jumped out, looking around warily. He wore a pale-blue button-down shirt tucked neatly into perfectly creased tan pants and loafers with no socks. Rigidly straight black hair hung over his eyes, and he ran a hand across his forehead to push it away. His eyes narrowed as he surveyed the scene, but when no one else yelled at him, he visibly relaxed, the lines across his forehead and around his lips smoothing. He closed the car door and moved toward the coffee shop across the way.

A few feet from the car, he stopped, turned back, and called out, "Brad?"

A hand waved from the driver's side. Well, not so much waved as gestured. Whoever was inside said something in a harsh voice that didn't carry.

The young man said, "Right, sorry, Dr. Atherton…" The man glanced over and saw he had an audience gathered in front of the Magic Shop. "Never mind, I'll figure it out." He trotted into the coffee shop, his hands digging into his pockets.

"Brad?" Anna repeated, sharing a look with Sammy. She walked briskly to the sports car, leaning her hands on the open passenger-side window. "Are you Brad Atherton?"

The driver turned his head slowly and gave Anna a look that screamed disdain. "Yes. Who are you?"

"Hi, um," Anna stuttered. Now that she had the man in

front of her, she wasn't sure what she really wanted to ask. "I understand you're friends—I mean—you were friends with Oliver Humphreys-Gibbons."

Brad's hands, large enough that they covered most of the steering wheel, whitened as his grip tightened. He sniffed sharply and frowned. "That's right, and who are you?"

"Sorry, I'm Anna McGregor. I run a B and B in town."

Brad continued to stare at her.

"Right. So, um..."

A car came up the road behind them and honked, but Brad ignored it. The driver of the other car pulled forward cautiously, just barely managing to squeeze by Brad's car, which clearly blocked the lane.

Anna stood up straight. "I was hoping to talk with you, Brad. About Oliver, that is. I just have a few questions about him."

Brad raised his eyebrows. "Dr. Atherton."

"Oh, sorry."

"I don't know you, Ms. McGregor, and I have no idea why I would talk to you. Ah, Michael. Perfect timing."

The young man had returned from the coffee shop bearing two paper cups wrapped in cardboard protectors. "Here you go." He handed one in through the driver's-side window then walked around the car. When he reached for the passenger-door handle, however, Brad stopped him.

"I'll go alone, Michael. I don't need you hanging around the police station. Wait for me here."

"Right, sure." Michael stepped back from the car and waved his cup in a sort of salute as Brad revved the engine then sped off up the street, well above the posted speed limit. "Huh." Michael glared at his cup, walked to a nearby trash can, and tossed it in. Dusting off his hands, he seemed to notice Anna for the first time. "Can I help you?"

"Hi. I'm Anna McGregor. I was hoping to talk with Brad, but he seemed to be in a bit of a hurry. Going to the police station, right?"

Michael's eyes narrowed again. "Why do you want to talk to Dr. Atherton?"

Anna offered as friendly a smile as she could muster. "You're a student of his, right?"

Michael nodded, but his expression remained wary.

"I used to work in the anthro department there. I don't think we've ever met, though."

Michael's eyes lit with recognition. "Anna McGregor. I should have recognized the name. Sure. I know all about you."

Anna frowned. That didn't sound good.

❧ 20 ☙

"So tell me. What have you heard?" Anna asked, once all the introductions had been made between Anna, Sammy, and Michael Chan, who Anna learned was a fifth-year graduate student in linguistics. They strolled slowly up and down Washington Street, avoiding other pedestrians.

"About you?" Michael grinned. "You're a bit of a hero."

Anna's mouth opened in surprise.

"She is?" Sammy put Anna's thoughts into words. "You're kidding."

"Sure." Michael shrugged. "We always work with faculty on their research while they get most of the credit."

"That's not actually true," Anna pointed out. "Honest professors include their students as co-authors on their papers."

"I know, I know, but what about the ideas? I had this brainstorm last year that led to a whole new approach in our lab, but Brad still got credit as the principal researcher when we published the work." Michael's voice took on a whiny edge.

"So, you know about Steve and what he did?" she redirected Michael before he could turn the conversation into a venting session.

Michael nodded vigorously. "Oh, yeah. The school said he's on sabbatical this year, but we all know he's in the doghouse for trying to claim your research as his own. That's not cool."

"Good." Anna tried to stay serious, but she couldn't stop a smile from spreading across her face. "So, why are you and Brad in Cape May today?"

Michael lifted a shoulder in a shrug. "We didn't have to come. The cops said they could talk to Brad in Philly, but he insisted on coming down. He said this was a big deal. Oliver was his partner, blah blah blah. As if."

"As if what?" Anna asked, puzzled.

Michael's lips pulled into a tight line, and he took a moment before responding. "Oliver was a great linguist, one of the best. Brad was jealous of him. I'm sure of it. Brad never appreciated how much he benefitted from working with Oliver."

"Then why did you come with him?" Sammy asked.

"He likes to have a student around, for when he needs something," Michael answered, one side of his mouth turning up into a crooked grin. "You know, like coffee."

Anna rolled her eyes. That wasn't right.

"You came down with him to get him coffee?" Sammy repeated, one eyebrow raised.

This time Michael grinned for real. "Nah, not really. I just... I loved Oliver, you know?"

Both women looked at him.

"I mean, I really respected him and what he was doing. I hate that he's dead. And to think I was down here when..."

"You were in Cape May earlier this week?" Anna asked. "Did you see Oliver?"

Michael shook his head. "I'm surprised I didn't. I expected to see him at dinner. Brad had invited some funders, you know? He took them out to a nice dinner then invited them back to his boat for drinks afterward. Oliver should have been there. Even Tara Blanch came."

"You know Tara Blanch?"

"Sure. Everyone does. A lot of people think she's on a short list for a Nobel Prize for her writing. She's amazing."

"Hmph." Anna thought of the irritable woman locked away in her room. "She may be a great writer, but she's not very personable."

"Nah, that's just when she's focused. She has amazing focus. You should have seen her at dinner that night. Friendly, chatting away. She has some crazy ideas about the way the world works, the way people act and think. That's why she's so interested in linguistics and why she got along so well with Oliver." Michael furrowed his brow and shook his head. "Except Oliver wasn't there."

"Maybe he had other plans," Anna suggested.

"Or he was already dead," Sammy pointed out.

Michael shuddered visibly and closed his eyes. "Please don't say that."

Anna considered the young man next to her. He said he loved Oliver for his research, for his knowledge, but maybe something else was going on as well. Maybe Michael's feelings had been more than just professional.

"Plus, there's the fishing."

Michael's unexpected comment roused Anna from her thoughts. "What? Fishing?"

Michael's grin cut across his face, and his eyes lit up. "It's summer flounder season, and they can be a kick to catch." He rubbed his hands together as he spoke. "I can't wait to hit the water."

"So you have your ulterior motives too?" Sammy narrowed her eyes.

Michael shrugged. "Sure, why not? I love fishing—the open water, the fight against the fish. No intellect, no fancy arguments, just pure power. Hey, if Brad can take advantage of my time, then so can I."

"Of course, I think that's—"

An extended, ear-splitting honk cut Anna off.

The red car had returned, and Brad did not look happy.

"Gotta run." Michael didn't even look back as he dashed to Brad's side.

"Well, that's what he gets for taking a free ride to get some fishing in." Sammy shook her head. "I guess nothing is really free. Is it?"

Anna rolled her eyes. "Come on. We better hurry. Beth-Anne and Eoin will be waiting for us." She grabbed her friend's hand and trotted toward the restaurant. She couldn't resist a look back, however.

Michael sat silently in the passenger seat, occasionally nodding, while Brad gesticulated wildly, swerving to narrowly avoid pedestrians as he drove.

What a pair. Anna stopped suddenly, pulling Sammy to a halt with her.

"What? What happened?" Sammy asked.

Anna laughed. "I totally forgot to ask him about how well Steve knew Oliver. That was why I wanted to talk to Brad in the first place."

＃ 21 ＃

nna hung the final clean mug on the line of hooks in the dining room and tossed the dishcloth over her shoulder, finishing the breakfast cleanup. It was time to clean the rooms. She shook her head and laughed to herself as she considered how much of her new life entailed cleaning. She just needed to get her work out of the way so she could focus on finding out more about Oliver and those who knew him.

"Cousin Anna! Cousin Anna!" Eoin burst into the dining room and slid to a stop a few inches shy of the dish cabinet.

"Whoa." Anna put out a hand to support him. "What's got you so excited?"

Eoin's eyes glowed. "BethAnne is here." The words came out in his quiet whisper, imbuing the name with a sense of awe.

"Aha." Anna tried to keep a serious expression but turned away from him when she realized she couldn't keep it up. She understood what it meant to have a crush on someone. No way would she let Eoin see her making light of it. "Is she outside? I'll bring out some lemonade."

"She has a friend." Eoin spun and ran back out to the porch.

Curious what that might mean, Anna piled four glasses and a pitcher of lemonade on a tray and followed the sound of voices out to the porch. The chattering stopped as Anna came outside. Three sets of eyes turned toward her. Three mouths pinched shut.

Anna raised an eyebrow. "Good morning, BethAnne. It's good to see you." She placed the tray on a side table and passed around each glass as she filled it from the pitcher.

"Thanks, Ms. McGregor." BethAnne took her glass and handed another to the boy sitting next to her. "This is my friend, David."

"Hello, David. Nice to meet you." Anna noticed that Eoin had somehow managed to squeeze between BethAnne and David where they sat on the porch steps. She handed him his lemonade then stepped down to lean against the bottom railing so they could face her comfortably. "What brings you around?"

Eoin kept his admiring gaze on BethAnne. BethAnne looked steadfastly at David. David said nothing, his narrow shoulders hunched under his thin T-shirt, his worn sneakers peeking out from the bottom of his frayed jeans.

Finally, BethAnne turned to Anna. "I did some more reading about linguistics yesterday, after you left. It's super cool." She took a sip of lemonade, keeping a sideways glance on David. When he still said nothing, BethAnne continued, "I don't suppose Tara Blanch is around today. Is she?"

"I suppose she might be." Anna thought about how she'd avoided talking to the grumpy woman at breakfast that morning. "I should warn you, she's not the most... well, the most talkative person."

BethAnne shrugged. "That's okay. I just want to get her autograph, anyway. I'm sure she's busy."

Anna grinned at BethAnne's insight. She was a wise young woman, for sure. "So, what did you read about linguistics?"

"Just about the basics, current research, new technology, that sort of thing."

Anna laughed. "Right. Typical teenager reading. It's true. A lot of new technology is used these days. Personally, though, I preferred working with people in the field."

"In the field? What does that mean?"

Anna glanced at David, who still sat silently, his eyes on his now-empty glass of lemonade. "Oh, you know, going out into the neighborhoods where I was doing my research, talking to actual people about what they eat, where they shop. And not just asking them but spending time with them so I could see it for myself, understand for myself. That's what anthropology is."

"Huh. Do linguists do that too?"

"They can, yes. But as you've been reading, it can also be more lab based." She finished her own lemonade and put the glass down on the bottom step, leaning forward toward the youngsters. "Now, I don't think you two came here to talk about linguistics, did you?"

BethAnne shook her head and glared at David. "David, you're going to have to speak."

The silent boy looked up at Anna, and she straightened in surprise when she saw his expression. Creases better suited to an old man crept across his forehead. His mouth was pinched into a tight circle, and unshed tears gathered in his eyes. Was it guilt? Or fear? Or both?

"David, are you all right? Do you need help?"

He shook his head, shrugged, then dropped his gaze again.

BethAnne let out a loud sigh. "Fine, I'll tell you. David was out fishing in his little rowboat late Wednesday night, in Spicer Creek, where that man was found."

"Oh my." Anna put a gentle hand on David's shoulder. "Did you see anything? Did anyone see you?"

David's eyes opened wide. "See me? I hope not."

"He wasn't supposed to be out there," BethAnne explained. "He doesn't have a fishing license."

"I see." Anna nodded. "So you were fishing without a license, at night. What did you see, David?"

"I didn't see anything, but I heard it. I heard a noise, like people shuffling their feet, you know? It got really silent, then I heard a splash, a big one."

Anna's hand flew up to cover her mouth. Could David have heard Oliver going into the water?

"Have you told the police about this?"

"He won't," BethAnne replied. "Because of the license thing, because he knows he shouldn't have been out there."

"When BethAnne said she knew you, I thought maybe you could help." David looked up at Anna hopefully. "Since you were involved last time someone died in town, I thought..." His voice trailed off, and he raised his eyebrows.

"Oh, David, BethAnne. I'm glad you came to me. I really am. But only because you have to tell the police what you heard. I don't know what you think I can do."

BethAnne bristled. "Just cause we're kids doesn't mean we don't know what's going on around town. We hear things."

Eoin's blush told Anna he'd been talking to BethAnne about Anna's involvement in the previous case, possibly even bragging.

"Yeah," David chimed in, "like how you're really the one

who figured out who killed that man who died in your house."

BethAnne nodded, her beads bouncing.

"It's true," Anna admitted. "I have worked with the police, but that's how I know that you need to tell them what you heard."

David shuffled his feet. "I may have a few other reasons why I don't want to."

Anna couldn't imagine what else the boy was hiding, but she also knew he had no choice. "David, this could be vital information. What you heard—"

"Yoo-hoo!"

Anna spun around. She'd been so focused on BethAnne and David that she hadn't even heard Mrs. James coming up the front path.

"Mrs. James. Hi... uh... how are you?"

"I'm fine, dear. I just came to tell you..." She paused and glanced over both shoulders. "I heard that you have a very special guest staying with you this week."

"You did?"

Mrs. James nodded eagerly. "That writer... you know..."

Anna sighed. "You mean Tara Blanch. How did you hear she's here?"

Mrs. James leaned in closer. "I heard she's traveling under an assumed name—to keep her privacy."

"If that's true, then I really can't confirm it, can I?"

Mrs. James's lips pursed into a frown. "No, I suppose not. Well. I just wanted to let you know. That's all. I *thought* you might be interested." She looked down her nose at the children. "And you two shouldn't be sitting here, gossiping about things you're not supposed to."

Ha! Anna couldn't swallow her laugh in time. Talk about the pot calling the kettle black. But as she waved good-bye to Mrs. James, she had to wonder. How much had she over-heard? Whatever she'd overheard would soon be public knowledge, and that could put David in danger.

❧ 2 2 ❧

Anna's phone rang just as she reached for it. Her call to Evan to let him know about David's news would have to wait.

"Kathy," she answered after seeing the caller ID. "How are you? I was just about to make a call." She walked outside as she spoke. The teenagers still sat on the porch steps. They spoke in quick whispers but sat back and sipped innocently on their refilled lemonades as soon as she came out.

After exchanging a few pleasantries, Kathy said, "Are you still looking for information about the man who was killed?"

"I am. Why? What have you heard?"

"I wasn't digging for gossip, you understand." Kathy's reluctance was evident in her voice, and Anna could imagine her stern expression. "I meant what I said before. You really should leave it to the police."

"I know. You're right. But sometimes the information comes to me all on its own." She looked at David as she spoke, who smiled shyly then looked away.

"Huh. I don't know what that means. But the truth is I did find out something about the dead man, Oliver."

"Really? How? From whom?"

"Don't get so excited. It's nothing to do with his murder. It's something that happened a while ago."

"It's clearly something you think is relevant, so spill." Anna regretted pushing Kathy like that. She didn't want to scare her off.

Kathy's voice softened, however, and Anna realized she'd misread her friend's reluctance. "I just don't want to upset you. Felicia told me about what you've been through."

"Me? Why would I get upset?"

"Okay." Kathy took a deep breath. "It seems that, overall, Oliver was quite a stickler for the rules. He rubbed a number of people the wrong way by correcting them, even in public. But there was one area where he seemed willing to break the rules."

"Uh-oh," Anna said.

"Yes, that's right. He had a relationship with a student."

Anna shut her eyes, trying not to get upset. "One of his own students?"

"No, it was a young man from another department—no direct student–teacher relationship, but it still made for juicy gossip. Not just their relative positions in the university but also the fact that they're both men."

"Why would that matter?"

Kathy was silent for a moment before responding. "It still matters to some people, dear. I'm glad you're not one of them. Now tell me, did I do the right thing by telling you this?"

"Yes, you did. Thank you. How did you even find out?"

"To be honest, it just came up. I was chatting with friends over breakfast, down at the boathouse, and I mentioned that you were curious about the recent murder. No one was surprised, by the way."

"Yeah, I'm beginning to realize that everyone thinks of me as an amateur detective these days."

"Right. That's not a good reputation to get, Anna. Please be careful. Anyway, when I mentioned your name, one of my friends said that it made sense you'd be curious because of the connection to the university, and he just mentioned the affair in passing."

Anna thanked Kathy and hung up the phone, thinking. What if Oliver's murder was actually a hate crime? Or a crime of passion? She shook her head. Just because the man was in a relationship didn't mean that was why he was killed.

"You all right, Cousin Anna?" Eoin had sidled over to her while she was on the phone, and he put a hand on her hip.

She grabbed his hand and squeezed tight. "I am, sweetheart. Thank you. And thank you both, too, for doing the right thing. I'm going to call Patrolman Burley right now."

❧ 23 ❧

"**M**s. McGregor?"

Anna tucked her phone into her pocket as she came back out to the porch. "Yes, BethAnne?"

"Did you tell the police about what David heard?"

"I did." She looked back and forth between the two teens. "I told Patrolman Burley everything you told me, but it's not good enough. They're going to have to talk to you directly, David. They can't just take my word for what you heard."

David leaned forward and pulled at the grass beside the porch. "Will I get in trouble?"

Anna sat beside him and put an arm around his shoulders. "I don't know, but I doubt it. The police will only talk to you while your parents are around. They won't try to catch you on your own or anything like that, and your parents will be there to make sure everything is okay."

David sighed. "My parents don't know I was out fishing."

"Oh. I see. David, you're being very brave. I hope you

understand that. A lot of people in your position wouldn't have said anything. But you're smarter than that, aren't you?"

"He sure is," BethAnne agreed. "There's nothing David can't do when he wants to."

Anna didn't doubt it. The boy didn't look particularly brave, crouching on the porch steps, picking at the grass. But he was friends with BethAnne, and that meant he must be smart and ambitious. Too bad he was a bit of a rule breaker.

Evan had responded positively to the news about David. The police would reach out to David's parents that afternoon and arrange a time when they could all meet as soon as possible. Anna had also taken the opportunity to remind Evan he needed to interview Steve.

"So..." BethAnne leaned forward to look around Anna to David. "Now that that's settled, can we meet Tara Blanch?"

Anna laughed out loud. "I don't know about that, Beth-Anne. I tried to talk to her yesterday morning, and she was not particularly interested."

"Sure. Right. Focused on her writing. I know. But like I said, I just want to get her autograph." BethAnne reached into her large backpack and pulled out a tattered paperback book.

"Is that from the library?" Anna asked.

BethAnne shook her head. "I bought it at the used bookstore. It's fabulous." Her eyes glowed as she described the book. "It's a collection of short stories, each about a different place, like different planets and stuff, and how each group of people has different laws and different ways of doing things. Sometimes they're scary. Sometimes they're sad. It's really good."

"I'm constantly impressed by you, BethAnne. You're

reading far ahead of your grade level. Okay." Anna stood. "You deserve a chance to meet this author. Let's see if we can find her."

Anna, BethAnne, David, and Eoin trooped up the stairs, creating quite a racket. Anna didn't mind. She thought it might be helpful to give Tara Blanch a heads-up that they were coming.

"Ms. Blanch?" Anna called out as she rapped on the bedroom door. "I'm sorry to bother you again. It's Anna McGregor, and I have some friends who'd really like to meet you."

The door flung open once again, and Anna found herself confronted by Tara Blanch's frowning features once more.

When the writer saw the children, however, her expression changed. "Is that my book?" She pointed at Beth-Anne's hands.

"It is." BethAnne nodded vigorously, her beaded braids clacking. "I loved it. Will you sign it for me?" She held the book out in both hands, as if making an offering to the writer.

"My dear, how old are you?"

"I'm sixteen."

"Oh my. Well, you better come in." Tara stepped back from the door to allow them all to crowd into the room. Tara moved to stand by the desk near the window. Eoin and David propped themselves against the bed. Anna slid into the rocking chair, and BethAnne stayed in the middle of the room. "I didn't expect to meet a fan of your age."

BethAnne blushed. "I've been told I'm precocious." She looked down at the book. "But you will sign it for me, won't you?"

"I could do no less." Tara smiled, reached across to the

desk for a pen, and took the book from BethAnne. "Now, who should I make this out to?"

While BethAnne spelled out her name, Anna surreptitiously examined Tara's room. It was generally neat, no clothes, makeup, or other toiletries strewn about. But the neatness stopped at the desk, which was covered with papers, notebooks, and other books. From her angle, Anna could make out the names of Labov, Bourdieu, and a few other linguists Anna was familiar with.

"I see you're reading up on linguistics," Anna commented. "BethAnne is quite knowledgeable on that topic as well."

Tara's brow lowered for a moment as she glared at Anna, then she looked back at BethAnne, and her expression cleared. "That's lovely, dear. I hope you're able to keep up all of your reading. I write fiction, of course, but everything I write is well grounded in reality and current research."

"I heard that you were friendly with Oliver Humphreys-Gibbons and Brad Atherton." Anna tried to sound casual, but Tara glared at her again.

"I don't think that's any of your business." She kept her voice and face calm, but the words were clear. Tara turned back to BethAnne. "I'm sorry, dear. I'm a bit of an introvert. I suppose most of us writers are." She giggled.

"That's okay. I won't bother you. Thanks so much for the signature." BethAnne waved the book at Tara as she gestured for David and Eoin to leave the room ahead of her.

Anna waited until the three children were out of the room before turning back to Tara. "I'm sorry that I'm prying, but I know you spent time with Brad on his boat. Steve Upton mentioned that you were friends." Anna shrugged. "It's a small town. Word gets around. I just wondered if you had any insight into why Oliver might have been killed."

"I have insight on a great many things," Tara spoke through tight lips. "But I share that insight in my books, not in gossip. Yes, I joined Brad for dinner the other night. But that hardly makes me a witness to Oliver's murder. He wasn't even with us that evening. And before you ask, I don't know where he was."

Anna opened her mouth to ask another question, but Tara cut her off.

"I've had enough. If you can't leave me alone, I will have to find another place to stay."

Anna shut her mouth and nodded. "Of course. Thank you. Sorry." She left, pulling the door shut behind her. If Tara wouldn't talk, then Anna needed to find someone who would.

A nna caved and allowed Eoin to join BethAnne as she walked David home. She trusted the teenagers to keep an eye on the eight-year-old. Anna headed in the opposite direction, toward the marina. She didn't know if Brad would be there, but it was the only place she could think of to look for him.

A squat, two-story building guarded the entrance to the piers of the Cape May Marina, but Anna could see well enough from the walkway along the parking lot. Unlike some of the other marinas in the area, this one offered no pool to cool off in after a day on the boat. The people who used these boats didn't come back hot and tired. They returned relaxed and refreshed. About ten yachts lined the pier. If she was seeing clearly, one of the boats had its own pool, or maybe that was a hot tub.

Anna walked over to peer in the window of the guard-house. Clubhouse was more like it, definitely a clubhouse. The entrance was somewhat shielded by a cluster of potted ferns, but stepping back a bit, Anna could see in through a window. A long bar followed one wall. A few tall stools had been placed along it, but most of the seating came in the form of leather armchairs, which clustered in groups of three or four around low glass tables. A fireplace stood out on a far wall. It wouldn't be necessary at this time of year, but Anna could imagine it provided a perfect atmosphere for the club.

A few patrons sat comfortably sipping on Bloody Marys and mimosas.

She walked back along the path, studying each craft but trying not to be obvious in the process. The peaceful clink of sails and masts added a rhythmic background to the cries of the gulls overhead.

Half of them looked empty, but on the others, Anna saw people setting up the boats. On one, two young men dressed in white button-down short-sleeve shirts and white shorts wiped down every surface and set up chairs and tables on the deck. They were crew, clearly, hired to staff the boat.

Some of the people lounging on the boats looked like owners, enjoying a quiet Sunday morning, lounging in the sun. Maybe waiting for friends to join before setting off for the day.

Movement inside the eighth boat caught her eye. She saw a shadow move behind the large square windows that lined the boat's main cabin. She leaned forward on the railing, peering into the window to see if she knew the person inside. She already recognized the name of the boat. It belonged to Brad Atherton.

"Can I help you?"

Anna jumped and spun around. A man stood watching her, his eyes narrowed suspiciously. Or perhaps he looked like that from squinting in the sun. Anna couldn't be sure. Stubble covered his lower face, dark stubble that matched his hair, almost black but not quite. Long lashes shielded his dark eyes, and he wore his sleeves rolled up, revealing muscular forearms and part of a tattoo that ran down his arm. The gravel in his voice suggested he might be a smoker, but what surprised Anna more than that was his English accent.

"Oh. Hello. Sorry, yes. I'm Anna McGregor. I run a B and B in town."

The man continued to eye her but said nothing more.

"I'm looking for Brad Atherton," Anna continued, forcing herself to smile. "I know that's his boat, so I thought I might catch him here."

"He's not here," the man replied. "I don't know where he is."

Anna glanced back at the boat. "But someone's in there. Are you sure it's not him?"

"Said so, didn't I? It's not my job to track his movements, but I know he's not here."

"I see. And what is your job?"

"I'm the manager, aren't I?"

"Um, I don't know. Are you?"

The man glowered at her, his eyes narrowing even more. "I just said so, didn't I? Dennis Meakin. I'm here every day, all day, so if I say someone's not around, he's not around."

Anna glanced back at the boat then back at Dennis. "I'm sorry. I didn't mean to doubt you. Um, tell me, what exactly does a marina manager do?"

"Do?" Dennis's eyes opened wide, and Anna saw they were actually dark blue, not brown. "I do what needs to be done."

"So you deal with the owners of these yachts a lot, then?"

"Nah, not really. It's not my job to make the toffs happy. That's what the staff is for, to serve the blighters, clean up after them. My job is to make sure their boats are safe and the marina is clean and well cared for."

"And you're doing a good job." Anna scanned up and down the pier. "It looks great."

"Yeah, well it would, wouldn't it? I take my job seriously, particularly when a wild-looking woman comes around, peeking into people's private boats."

Anna brushed a hand over her mop of red hair, aware it had been blown into a mess by the seaside wind. "Right. Sorry about that. Like I said, I'm just looking for Brad, but if you say he's not here..."

Dennis took a step toward her, pushing his sleeves higher up his arms. "How many times do I gotta tell you?"

"Anna."

Anna let out her breath and spun around with relief. Michael Chan stood on the deck of the boat, waving at her. "What are you doing here?"

"Michael. Hi. I was looking for Brad." She glanced back at Dennis. "Or for you. Are you free to talk?"

"Me? Why? I mean, sure. I guess. Come on board."

"Hmph," Dennis grunted with distaste, but nevertheless, he opened the gate to allow Anna down onto the gangplank.

Anna thanked him brightly and trotted over to Brad's boat, taking Michael's hand as he helped her aboard.

❧ 25 ❧

Polished mahogany tables and cabinets glowed. Brass fittings shone in the bright noonday sun that filtered through the wide windows and reflected off the water around the boat.

"Wow! This is amazing." Anna took in the surprisingly large room. A sofa ran along one wall under a row of windows, curving around at the back of the room to create a low wall between this room and the galley behind it. It seemed like more of a wet bar, really, than a kitchen. Though fully fitted out, it didn't look like anyone had been cooking in it. Through the kitchen, Anna saw steps leading down to what she assumed was a sleeping area. Everything was scrubbed until it gleamed.

"It's a nice boat." Michael swept a pile of papers off the table and shoved them into a briefcase.

"But how can it be so big in here?"

"Bigger on the inside than the outside?" Michael laughed. "No such luck. It's just that a lot of the space is actually below water. Plus, she's one of the smaller yachts at this marina, so she probably looks small in comparison to the others. Berth this boat in the Bluff Point Boatyard, and you'd think differently. I'll just file these downstairs, and I'll be right back."

"Wow," Anna repeated, turning in a circle to see everything. And if Michael was filing papers downstairs, more than just bedrooms were down there.

"Sorry about that," Michael said as he came back up. "Brad's turned one of the cabins into an office. Well, office-slash-den. It's all fitted out with a TV, sound system, gaming console, the works."

"*One* of the cabins? How many are there?"

Michael laughed but didn't answer, stepping into the galley. "Can I offer you some water or coffee or tea?" As he spoke, he bent down and pulled open cabinet doors, looking to see what else he had to offer. "Well, will you look at that?"

He straightened, holding a half-empty bottle of liquor, his brows lowered and his lips pulled into a tight line.

"What's that?"

"Gin."

"Oh. Is Brad not supposed to have alcohol on here?" Anna asked. "But didn't he just have people over for a cocktail? Maybe that's just left over?"

"That jerk. Why did he...?" Patches of pink and red appeared on Michael's cheeks as he seemed to search for words. His grip on the bottle tightened until Anna worried he would shatter the neck.

"Michael, is everything okay?"

Michael glared at the bottle for a second longer then looked up at Anna. His expression lightened as if he'd just remembered she was there. "Sorry, he just makes me so angry sometimes."

"Who, Brad? I don't get it."

"This bottle"—Michael waved the bottle at her as he

spoke—"he sent me out to get something he already had right here. That's just like him not to look around first, just call on me and get me to fix it. Even if I'm already doing something else for him, like tending to his funders."

"Sorry." Anna grimaced. "Brad's a big drinker, huh? I wouldn't have guessed that."

"Ha, no. He just loves this one cocktail. He likes to serve it when he has guests over, like the other night with the funders. He told me he needed gin and asked me to stop at the liquor store on the way over with his guests. So I did, but it looks like he was just wasting my time."

Anna felt bad for Michael but wasn't surprised. It seemed perfectly in character for Brad from what she'd learned about him so far. His first priority was himself and his comfort, even if it meant making other people do unnecessary work, other people like Michael. "What's the cocktail?"

"It's called a Bee's Knees." Michael turned back to search through the cabinets. "Let's see. Gin, honey simple syrup, lemon juice..." He pulled small bottles out as he spoke.

Anna made a face. "Ew, that sounds awfully sour."

"Oh no, it's really good." Michael raised one eyebrow, and Anna saw an evil glint in his eye. "Want to try one?"

"Now? It's only just noon!"

"Come on. We're on a yacht on a glorious Sunday in June. Let's relax." Michael started pouring ingredients into a cocktail shaker and gestured Anna toward the deck at the back of the boat.

As she settled onto the narrow bench, Michael came out and handed her a martini glass filled with a yellow drink.

"Cheers." Michael held up his glass and took a sip.

Anna sipped hers tentatively then, surprised, took another sip. "You're right. That is good."

Michael nodded and leaned back on a bench across from her. The deck wasn't as big as the great room inside, but the sliding glass door stood wide open, making it feel like it was all part of the same room. Their benches sat under a canvas awning, keeping the sun off their heads, for which Anna was grateful. They sat in silence for a moment, and Anna enjoyed the sound of the water lapping against the hull of the boat, the gentle rock of the tide, the sweet-and-sour taste of her drink.

She closed her eyes and leaned back. "I could live like this."

"Yeah, so could I." Michael's voice carried more than a note of cynicism.

"But seriously, how can Brad afford this?"

"Family money. Trust me. He's not even a full professor yet. No way he could afford this on his own."

"Ah." Anna nodded. "Nobody goes into academics for the money, do they?"

Michael grinned and raised his glass in agreement. "Though Brad does pretty well with his funding, I gotta admit. He's built a state-of-the-art linguistics lab, you know. I don't know if you were ever there."

Anna shook her head, so Michael went on to tell her about the various high-tech tools Brad had accumulated over the years, thanks to the support he'd gained from federal, state, and private funding sources. From microphones and recording equipment to a sound-attenuated booth, an ultrasound, and electroglottograph for measuring voice quality and the movement of vocal flows. Anna lost track after a while and just nodded as Michael spoke, thinking that BethAnne might be more impressed with the list than she was. But Michael was clearly proud of it, and presumably so was Brad.

"Oliver Humphreys-Gibbons worked in that lab with Brad, too, right?" she finally interjected, breaking the flow of Michael's recitation.

"Oliver? Yeah." Michael nodded. "They shared management of the lab. Both brought in funding. Both got to make purchasing and management decisions. Actually, I think Oliver used it more than Brad did." He looked down into his glass, his eyes shielded from Anna's view. "He was a great linguist, a great scholar."

"I'm so sorry for your loss." Anna could think of nothing better to say. "At least his research survives him, right? His books, his articles. And you must have learned so much from him."

Michael looked past Anna to the bay behind her. He nodded but didn't say anything.

"Do you know his boyfriend?" Anna kept her voice casual.

Michael's head snapped toward her. "His boyfriend? Who told you about that?"

Anna shrugged. "Just some gossip I overheard. Sorry. Is it meant to be secret?"

"Not really." Michael raised one hand then let it fall limp in his lap. "It's just not common knowledge. At least that's what I thought. Oliver didn't like it when Brad or I mentioned it. I guess he was just sensitive about it, his partner being a student and all. Even Tara made him mad when she asked about it."

"That surprised you?"

Michael nodded. "They were good friends. Tara used to pick Oliver's brain all the time to find out the latest thinking about language and how it works and how people think about it." A sad smile cut across Michael's face then vanished just as quickly. "She's going to miss him too. Ha!" He barked out a laugh. "I don't see Brad being quite as helpful."

"I think it's great that someone who writes literature is so deeply engaged in the science of her subject," Anna said. "I would help her if I could."

"You miss it. Academics. Research." Michael said it as a statement, not a question.

"Yeah, I guess I do."

"So, why don't you come back?"

Anna laughed lightly as she thought about her outbursts when she left the department. "I may have burned some bridges when I left."

"Nah, I wouldn't worry about that." Michael gestured with his glass, and some of the yellow drink spilled onto the canvas-covered bench. "From what I hear, everyone knows the truth of the situation. I'm sure if you made a few calls, you could come back."

Anna spun her glass between her fingers then finished off the last of the drink. "I am still in touch with two of my committee members, just as friends," she added with a wry grin.

"Look, you made a mistake."

"That much is clear."

"But don't let that ruin your life."

"You think my life is ruined?"

"Sorry. I mean... I don't know. You act like you miss your studies. Do you want to go back?"

"Sometimes. It's not so easy. I loved doing the research. I loved spending all my time learning, studying, thinking. You know?"

"I do. Not only do we get to spend our efforts on something that intrigues us, but we get paid for it too."

"On the other hand, it wasn't perfect. It was stressful to

constantly work on grant applications, write articles, and submit conference papers."

"So, are you saying you're happier now?"

Anna opened her eyes wide in surprise. "That's exactly it. I loved that job more, but I'm happier now. Is that crazy?"

"Kind of." Michael laughed and got up to make himself another drink. "Maybe I just don't understand. Want another?"

"No thanks. One's enough for me." Anna followed him in to set her glass down in the small sink. Michael moved it into a dishwasher that blended in with the other cabinets. "Seriously? A dishwasher? On a boat?"

"I know, I know. Like I said, family money. And he has even more of it now, since Brad's father cut off one of his other sons."

"What? What happened?"

Michael shrugged. "I don't know. It was stupid. Brad's brother dropped out of school—or failed out, is what Brad says. Anyway, their dad said he'd embarrassed him, embarrassed the whole family, and he cut him off."

"Just like that?"

"Just like that." Michael had been focused on measuring out his cocktail. He raised his eyes to look at Anna. "No second chances for him."

"You said earlier that I shouldn't let one mistake ruin my life. You believe in second chances?"

"Absolutely."

"So do I."

"Really? I wouldn't have thought that. You don't sound like you're going to give Steve Upton a second chance."

"Hey!" Anna laughed as she said it but was surprised at how well-informed Michael seemed to be. "That's none of your business, but since you ask, no, of course not. He's a liar and a thief."

"I know, I know. Sorry. You're right. It's none of my business." Michael poured his second drink into his glass, handed Anna a small bottle of water, and guided her back onto the deck.

"How well do you know Steve?" Anna asked.

"Not a lot. I mean, he spent time at the lab. He liked to think he was friends with Brad and Oliver."

"Liked to think?"

Michael laughed. "I don't think Brad has any friends, and I don't think Oliver ever really took him seriously as a researcher. He didn't do himself any favors, traipsing around after them like that."

Anna took a breath and looked around the boat, then back to the marina, trying to think of what else she could ask Michael. Movement on the pier caught her eye, and she looked in time to catch Dennis sliding behind a potted fern.

"That guy is creepy." She pointed toward Dennis with her bottle.

Michael turned in his seat to look where she pointed, but Dennis was hidden from view by then. "Who was it, Dennis?"

Anna nodded, taking another sip of water.

"Yeah, he's kind of weird, but he's a good guy. He set me up on a charter boat for tomorrow morning to do some fishing with a buddy of his, so that's good. Hey, why don't you come?"

"Fishing?" Anna's eyebrows shot up. "That's really not my scene."

"Oh, come on. You'll love getting out on the open water, feeling the wind in your hair, the heat of the battle as you go up against a powerful fish." Michael's hand tightened into a fist as he spoke, his eyes flashing.

"You really love it, don't you? Is this even a fishing boat?"

"This one? No, of course not. Dennis's friend has a boat, and he's taking a couple of other people out too. Come on, join me."

"I'm not sure. Look, thanks so much for the drink and the conversation." Anna stood, waving Michael back down when he moved as if to stand. "Don't worry. I'll see myself off, and I'll let you know about tomorrow morning, okay?"

"Okay, but not too late. We leave the marina at five."

26

Fishing, being out on the open water, wind in her hair, sun on her face—it sounded fabulous. But fishing.

Anna shook her head as she made her way slowly back to the center of town. She loved the idea of heading out on a boat, and she deserved some time off. What better way to spend a few hours on a beautiful morning? Plus, it would give her another chance to question Michael and learn more about Oliver, his life, and his friends, maybe even find out a bit more about Dennis, yet another mysterious character connected to boats. But she could admit that the idea of fishing did not entirely appeal to her.

She turned the corner onto Washington Mall, and her glance fell on two men sitting at a table outside the coffee shop across from the Magic Shop. Evan and Steve.

That was interesting. Hopefully, Evan had taken her concerns to heart and was seriously interviewing Steve about Oliver. Then again, if that was the case, why would they be out in the open, at a coffee shop?

"Hello, boys." Anna spoke with a fake drawl as she

approached their table. "Come here often?" She realized how ridiculous she sounded, and her cheeks burned. Perhaps that cocktail had affected her more than she realized. She coughed. "Sorry, just passing by. I thought I'd stop for a coffee."

Evan stood, but Steve stayed in his chair. "That's great, Anna," Evan said. "But you'll have to find another table. This is an official conversation."

"It is?" Anna's eyebrows shot up. "Oh. I see. Well..." She glanced around then back at Evan. "Okay then."

He waved tentatively as he sat back down, watching her.

Anna meandered over to the store immediately next to the coffee shop and pretended to be entranced by the display of children's toys in the windows. She was only about ten feet from the men but still had to focus to hear their words.

Evan spoke. "Tell me again, Mr. Upton. Why did you come to Cape May?"

"Because I heard about Oliver's death. I know it doesn't make any sense. Believe me, I regret it now."

Evan paused then lowered his voice. "So not because you wanted to see Ms. McGregor?"

"Well... yes, I was hoping to see her. I guess it seemed like a good opportunity."

Anna bit her lip to prevent a sound of disgust.

"A murder seemed like a good opportunity to catch up with your old girlfriend?" Evan asked, and Anna was glad to hear the disbelief in his voice.

A mother and two young children appeared next to Anna, laughing and pointing and talking about the toys on display. Their chatter drowned out Steve's response. That wasn't going to work. Anna trotted past the men's table and into the coffee shop. She might as well get that coffee.

Back outside, mocha latte in hand, Anna found an empty chair at a table only a few feet from Evan and Steve. She'd just sat down when she felt a hand on her arm.

"Not here, Anna." Evan held her gently but still somehow got her to stand. He led her a few feet away. "You really shouldn't be here. Not just because this is an official interview, but because your presence will affect how Steve answers. You must see that."

"Oh. I hadn't thought of that." Anna knew she was blushing again and put a hand up to her face. "I'm sorry. I guess I'm not very good at this, am I?"

Evan raised an eyebrow. "I hope it stays that way. I can't prevent you from sitting out here and enjoying your coffee, but please at least sit at a different table."

Anna grumbled but agreed. Weaving between the tables, she found a seat at the far edge of the cordoned-off patio and sat with her back to Evan and Steve. Guests chatted as they enjoyed their snacks, but snatches of Evan and Steve's conversation still made their way to her.

"I didn't know him that well," she heard Steve say. "I consulted with him a few times, sure. I'm familiar with his research. But we weren't social, if that's what you mean."

A few seconds later, she overheard a question from Evan. "Where were you on Thursday night?"

"I was in Philly, at home, alone. I considered dropping by a conference going on there."

Anna inhaled sharply. Steve had specifically told her he wasn't planning to attend the conference. When she heard the screech of the chair moving across the pavement, she knew she'd given herself away with her gasp. She was standing by the time Evan maneuvered through the tables to her.

"I know, I know. I'm leaving."

Evan's jaw moved, but he kept his mouth shut, clearly fighting the urge to say whatever was on his mind.

"I thought you should know I'm going fishing with Michael Chan tomorrow morning."

"You're what?" Even in his surprise, Evan sounded angry. "Why would you do that? He's connected to the victim. He might be..."

"Might be what?"

"Nothing. Just think about your actions, Anna, please. Be careful."

Anna glanced back and saw Steve watching them. She lowered her voice. "It might be a great opportunity to learn more about Oliver."

"That's exactly what I was thinking," Evan replied in an equally lowered voice. "Which is why it's not a wise move, is it?" He briefly shut his eyes, took a breath, then opened them and looked at Anna. "I have to get back to my inter-view. We'll talk about this later, okay?"

"Sure." Anna shrugged and grinned. Why not?

❧ 27 ❧

As usual, Eoin's eyes lit up as soon as Sammy appeared at Climbing Rose Cottage. He ran to greet her at the door, took her hand, and led her back to the kitchen, where he and Anna had been cleaning up after afternoon tea. Well, Anna had been cleaning. Eoin had been contributing to the mess—with nothing but the best intentions, of course.

"Grab a dishcloth," Anna greeted her friend with a grin. "You're just in time."

"Ugh, more washing." Sammy groaned but picked up the indicated towel and took her place next to Anna at the sink. "I only just finished cleaning up the bakery, you know."

"D'you want to see what I'm reading?" Eoin trotted up to Sammy with a book that required both his hands to hold. "It's about the Jersey Devil. It lives in the Pine Barrens, y'see, and it was the thirteenth son of a thirteenth son." His brow furrowed, and he looked over at Anna. "Why's the number thirteen so important, Cousin Anna?"

"It's just a ghost story, Eoin. Nothing is wrong with the number thirteen."

Sammy raised an eyebrow. "That depends on who you ask though, doesn't it? To some people, the number thirteen is very unlucky."

Eoin's eyes opened wide with wonder and curiosity. "Why?" He almost whispered the question.

"Oh. Er. Actually." Sammy giggled. "I don't really know."

"I think it comes from a number of different myths, different religions." Anna shrugged. "But like I said, don't let it scare you, Eoin. I'll have to take you to the Pine Barrens one of these days so you can see just how beautiful it is. Don't let the name fool you."

"Can we go now?" Eoin jumped up and down as he asked, and the heavy book slipped from his grasp, hitting the floor with a bang. He gasped, grabbed it off the ground, and carried it carefully over to the table while Anna and Sammy struggled not to laugh. "Can we go now?" he asked again once the book was safe.

"It's too late today, honey. Another weekend. But we can go somewhere closer, here in Cape May."

Sammy finished drying the last plate and hung up the dish towel, then turned to Anna. "You have somewhere specific in mind. Don't you?"

Anna gave her most innocent look. "It's still a beautiful afternoon. We should go look at the water, perhaps a marina?"

Eoin jumped again. "Boats! Yes! I have a book about boats!" he called as he ran out of the room.

"I sure hope it's not as big as his book about the Jersey Devil," Sammy said.

"He does love to read. Did I tell you that my mom confirmed his story about finishing the school year early?"

Sammy shook her head, her brow lowered in confusion. "What story?"

"Eoin came to Cape May to stay with me earlier than I expected because his school had a fire."

"That's terrible! I hope no one was hurt."

Anna shook her head. "I don't think so. But when his parents realized they would have to home school him for the rest of the year, they had a counselor meet with him. Eoin tested out of all his classes."

"Who can blame them?" Sammy laughed. "I wouldn't relish the idea of trying to teach Eoin anything."

"Right..." Anna looked around the kitchen one more time to make sure everything was clean and put away. "But that still doesn't explain why they sent him out here early. Why not just spend the extra time together?"

"You got me." Sammy shrugged. "I think that boy is a hoot."

Anna couldn't help but agree. Eoin's footsteps clattered down the stairs, making them both smile, and they ran out to the hall to meet him.

Ten minutes later, the three of them approached the Cape May Marina. Eoin had pulled the fortuitously small paperback book of boats out of his pocket and read as they walked. Anna had to keep one hand on his shoulder, redirecting him whenever he started wandering off the sidewalk, his focus on the book in his hand.

"Keep an eye out for a crazy-looking, dark-haired guy," Anna spoke under her breath to Sammy. "He's the manager here, and he's not super friendly."

"Got it. Crazy-looking, dark-haired guy." Sammy pulled a face. "Anything else I can go on?"

"He has an English accent, and he's the only person here who looks like he doesn't belong."

"Besides us, you mean?"

"Is that him?" Eoin's high-pitched voice cut through Sammy's quiet laugh.

Anna was surprised he'd been listening, she thought he was too focused on his book. She looked to where he pointed. He'd found Dennis, all right. And Dennis was being his typical creepy self.

"What's he doing?" Sammy asked.

"I can't tell." Anna shook her head, stepping behind a large potted plant so Dennis couldn't see her watching him.

Dennis moved along the pier, stopping at each boat. Every time he stopped, he poked around in the metal box that stood at the entrance to the dock then made a mark on the clipboard he carried.

"He's checking on the boats," Eoin said confidently. "It's his job."

"Hm," Anna wondered aloud. "Looks to me like he's searching for something."

"You're just saying that because you think he's creepy," Sammy replied. "I'm sure Eoin's right."

Eoin looked up at her, his eyes wide behind his round glasses. "Thank you, Sammy," he whispered, then added, "Eoin," correcting her pronunciation.

Sammy put an arm around him and pulled him close. "Now what, Anna? We just sit here behind this potted fern, watching?"

"I guess not. Can you tell if anyone is on Brad's boat? It's that one, second from the end."

Sammy leaned around the small tree to get a better view. Eoin leaned with her, his head poking out at half the height of hers.

"I can't tell from here."

"I can't tell either." Eoin shook his head.

"Something about Dennis just bugs me," Anna explained. "I mean, what's his deal? He takes this job but then gets annoyed by the people who own the boats. He complained to me about having to take care of them. So, why does he still work here?"

Sammy shrugged. "Not everyone gets to do what they want, you know. Maybe he's just glad he has a job."

"Maybe," Anna replied, but she wasn't convinced. "Or maybe he's finally snapped and is getting back at the 'toffs,' as he calls them."

They watched Dennis in silence for another minute or so as he made his way to the end of the pier.

"Michael Chan is going fishing tomorrow morning with a friend of Dennis's, and he invited me to go with them," Anna broke the silence.

"Fishing? You don't fish," Sammy pointed out.

"No. But this could be a chance to find out more about creepy Dennis."

"Is he going to be there?"

"I don't think so, but he's the one who set up the trip for Michael. It's his friend's boat."

"Are you going?"

Anna shrugged. "Yeah, I think so. Wanna come with me?"

"I'll come," Eoin answered for Sammy, but Anna shook her head.

"Sorry, I don't think that would be appropriate. I already checked with BethAnne, and she's available to come over tomorrow morning to watch you and serve breakfast to my guests."

Eoin's face had fallen when Anna first said no, but his crestfallen expression changed to excitement when she mentioned BethAnne, the other woman in his life.

"I don't know, Anna. I can't keep abandoning the bakery. I mean, my staff have been great in my absence, but how often can I leave them in charge?"

"Oh, come on, please?" Anna tugged at Sammy's sleeve. "You wouldn't leave me to do this on my own, would you? I told Michael I'd meet him at the Bluff Point Boatyard at five a.m."

"That late?" Sammy laughed.

Anna grimaced. "It may be fine for you, but you know that's way earlier than I usually start."

"I'll think about it." Sammy turned to look at Dennis again. He'd finished whatever he'd been doing and was slowly walking back down the pier, his eyes on the boats. At least he hadn't noticed them watching him.

Anna's phone rang, and she jumped, digging for it in her back pocket. Sammy ducked lower behind the potted tree, pulling Eoin down with her. "Shhh!"

"Sorry!" Anna whispered. She silenced her phone then saw who was calling. She slid away from Sammy and Eoin, toward the parking lot, and answered in a whisper. "Hi, Evan."

"Why are you talking like that?" Evan sounded so loud Anna pushed the phone tight against her ear and looked back. Dennis didn't seem to have noticed them, or if he had, he was politely ignoring them, which didn't seem like him.

"Like what?" Anna asked. "Oh, the whisper. No reason. I'm outside and don't want other people listening in."

She shrugged wildly at Sammy, who stifled a giggle and turned back to keep an eye on Dennis.

"I'm calling to talk to you about that fishing trip you mentioned. I know I said this before, but I got the impression you didn't agree with me. You really shouldn't go."

"I appreciate your concern, Evan, but I'll be perfectly safe."

"You don't know anything about these men, Anna. How can you even consider going off in a boat with them?"

"It's okay. Sammy will be with me."

Evan coughed a laugh. "Right, your bodyguard. And what exactly will she do to protect you?"

"I promise I'll be careful. I mean, what's he going to do in broad daylight, with other people around?"

Evan protested a few more times, but he must have realized he was fighting a losing battle.

Anna said goodbye and dropped the phone back into her pocket. Was Evan right? Was this crazy? She tiptoed back to Sammy and Eoin. "What's he doing now?"

"You know, you're right. He is really creepy," Sammy said. "He's just standing there, looking out at the bay."

"Does he know we're here?"

Sammy shrugged. "Probably. We're not exactly masters of stealth, are we?"

Eoin, who was jotting notes in his dog-eared notebook, nodded.

Anna laughed. "We need to learn more about him, then. What if he was somehow involved in the murder? He's got access to the boats. No one would think his being here at night was weird. We know he doesn't like 'toffs,' and it sounds like that description would fit Oliver perfectly."

"If he was involved in the murder"—Sammy shook her head—"then we should stay away."

"Then we need to find out," Anna corrected her.

Sammy sighed, and Anna knew she'd won.

It really was coldest before the dawn. Anna shivered and wrapped her wool sweater more tightly around herself, pulling her wool cap down over her ears. She stepped closer to Sammy, rubbing her arm against her friend's. "I'm so cold."

Sammy laughed. "It'll warm up when the sun comes up. Don't worry." Despite her brave words, she zipped her fleece jacket higher and stuck her hands into her pockets.

In the dim predawn light, Anna could just make out the far side of the bay as the boat passed out of the marina and turned toward the canal that would take them out to the ocean. A cold wind wrapped loose strands of her hair around her neck, and she hunched to protect herself. As the light grew, she identified more details on the passing banks—the branches of low, bent trees tangled with creeping vines, patches of water glistening among the reeds and mud.

"That's where they found his body, isn't it?" Sammy asked softly, pointing to a spot still marked off with yellow police tape.

The tape seemed unnecessary. Anna couldn't imagine anyone walking along that bank. "And the other body," Anna replied.

"Other body?"

"Apparently, another body was found in the same spot about fifty years ago. I don't know much about that story, but some of my neighbors use it as the basis for a ghost story. Something to scare visitors, you know?"

Michael had approached as she spoke about the ghost, and he laughed. "Ghosts. My God, people will do anything to make a buck. Won't they?"

"I think it's spooky," Sammy said. "What are the odds that a dead body would turn up in the same spot after fifty years?"

"Coincidence," Anna said firmly. "It must be coincidence and, like Michael said, people spinning the story to make it more interesting—something to sell to tourists."

"That's right." Michael put an arm around Anna's shoulders. "Coffee, ladies?"

"Please."

"Oh yes."

They bundled into the small cabin, where Captain Jessie had a pot of coffee brewing. Two other passengers left the cabin as they entered, tossing their paper coffee cups in the small trash can by the door as they went.

"It smells divine," Sammy said gratefully as she took her cup and looked around. "This boat isn't bad."

"Thanks." Jessie acknowledged the compliment but said no more, instead turning back to the helm.

"Don't worry about him," Michael interjected. "He's not much of a socializer."

"He's friends with Dennis, right?" Anna asked. "Not just some random stranger?"

Michael laughed. "Don't worry. He's fine. Yes, he's

friends with Dennis. I've actually met him once or twice before at the marina. You have nothing to worry about." He glanced around the small cabin as he spoke. "And you're right. This boat isn't bad. Nothing like Brad's, of course."

"Sammy, you should see that boat," Anna agreed. "It must be worth millions. It's amazing."

Sammy blew on her coffee then took a sip. "How can a professor afford something like that?"

"He's not even a full professor," Michael scoffed.

"Family money," Anna explained.

"He's always buying something," Michael added. "I would know. I'm always filling out the paperwork."

"Paperwork for his boat?" Sammy asked.

"Nah, not that. For the lab. He constantly has me file statements about how he's spending his grant money on new equipment."

"That's good, though, right?" Anna asked. "He's keeping the lab up-to-date."

Michael raised an eyebrow and shrugged. "You'd think, but I can't remember the last time I filed a receipt to close out the expenditure."

"I don't follow," Anna said, confused.

"I do." Sammy nodded. "Anytime I buy something for my bakery, I file the receipt to show that it was an actual business expense. But you can't file the receipt until you buy the item."

"But why would Brad have you fill out paperwork requesting grant funds then not buy that item?" Anna gasped as the full meaning hit her.

"Oh!" Sammy and Anna spoke at the same time.

Michael laughed and took a sip of his coffee. "I can't prove anything, you know. And it doesn't really matter."

"Doesn't matter?" Anna's voice rose in surprise. "He's embezzling funds from the grant, claiming to purchase items for the lab but not really purchasing them. How does that not matter?"

"Aren't there rules against that?" Sammy asked.

Michael shook his head. "It's just typical Brad. He's so picky when it's his own money, but when it's grant money, he doesn't really care. Maybe he eventually buys the equipment. Maybe he doesn't. He's all about spending other people's money." He shook his head again and laughed quietly. "But when it's his own money, forget it. Like when I went to pick up that gin for the Bee's Knees, it had to be Tanqueray."

He took a last slug of coffee then tossed the paper cup into the small trash can and headed back out onto the deck.

Sammy and Anna shared a look, shrugged, and followed Michael. They found him leaning against the deck railing, facing out toward the approaching ocean, his back to the canal they'd come through.

Sammy leaned next to him. "Why do you do those things for him? You're not his servant."

"What do you know about it?" Michael's eyes narrowed, and his lower jaw jutted out as he spoke. "You don't have the first clue what it's like to be a graduate student, constantly begging for money, for approval." He forcefully pushed back from the railing and turned his back to the women.

"Sorry," Sammy muttered. "I was just trying to help."

"Yeah, well, don't."

"It's okay, Michael. I totally get it. I do." Anna spoke softly, hoping to calm the angry man down—and return to the topic at hand. "Would Brad ever face any consequences for taking the grant money? If he didn't really buy the equipment, I mean. It sounds like it was in small amounts."

"It must add up over time, right?" Sammy asked.

Michael shrugged and leaned on the railing again. "No, no consequences. It's his money. No one's tracking it that carefully. If Oliver had noticed, he would've complained to Brad, and that's about it. Even if Oliver had submitted an official complaint to the funding organization, the most Brad would've gotten is a strongly worded letter telling him not to do it again."

He suddenly smacked the railing, and it vibrated under Anna's arms.

"Why are we even talking about this?" Michael spun toward them. "We're here to have fun. Right?" He hit the railing again and strode away toward Jessie.

"Whew! I didn't mean to make him so angry. I thought I was helping," Sammy said.

"I know, honey. You were trying to help." Anna put an arm around her friend, and they looked out to the ocean as the boat left the canal and entered the open sea. "Michael's clearly got a temper."

"And he's not Brad's fan."

Anna shook her head. "I almost wonder if he killed Oliver."

"That doesn't make any sense." Sammy twisted to look Anna in the face. "I could totally see Michael killing someone in anger, but it would've been Brad not Oliver."

Anna nodded, hugged her friend, then pushed up from the railing. "You're right. From everything I've heard, Oliver was basically a normal guy, trying to do the right thing and getting frustrated."

Sammy shrugged. "Maybe doing the right thing is what got him killed."

Anna looked back at Michael and Jessie, who were in the back of the boat, pulling together rods, reels, and bait. "At least Michael's calmed down a bit."

"Good. Let's keep him that way. Otherwise this will be a very bumpy ride."

29

"This isn't so bad. Is it?" Anna glanced at Sammy.

Sammy stood next to her on the deck at the stern of the boat, their rods trailing in the water. "As long as I don't get a bite." She grinned.

Captain Jessie had been good enough to bait their rods for them. Sammy refused to touch the slimy squid slices he used as bait. Anna didn't mind handling it but had no knowledge of how to get it on correctly. She was glad he'd done the work but worried that one of the fluke they were fishing for might actually take the bait. So far, they'd been lucky.

Michael, on the other hand, had caught a few already. He seemed to be on a roll. Despite his success, with every cast, he seemed to get more and more worked up.

Sammy nudged Anna. "I thought he liked fishing? Why does he do something that gets him so angry?"

"You got me. Maybe it's like how some people like to play violent video games because of the thrill. Michael did say he loved the fight. Maybe he's not really angry, just letting his aggression out. Personally, I always heard fishing was relaxing. For example, look at those two."

The two other fishermen on board had somehow managed to befriend Captain Jessie. The three of them huddled together on the far railing, laughing and drinking —coffee for Captain Jessie, beer for the other two.

"Ugh. How could they drink beer at this time of morning?"

Anna laughed. "I have no idea, but they're clearly getting into the spirit of things."

Captain Jessie pulled a small flask out of his pocket and tipped something into his coffee.

Anna frowned. "As long as we get home safely."

"Maybe that's the only way Captain Jessie can be friendly," Sammy suggested.

Anna agreed. She'd been unable to get more than two words out of him at a time. So much for finding out more about Dennis. "I guess I just need to relax and enjoy this. We only have one more hour out here." She leaned forward, tilted her face toward the sun, and closed her eyes.

The buzz from her pocket startled her. She must have left her phone on vibrate since yesterday. Maybe that was for the best, she thought, eyeing Michael. His aggression had surprised her. At least he was taking it out on the fish. He must have caught something again, because he shifted into a fighting stance, both hands on one of his rods.

She turned away from the men and leaned on the edge of the boat. She hadn't recognized the number. "Hello?"

"Anna?" Brooke's voice was immediately recognizable, and she was obviously distressed.

"Brooke, what's wrong? They haven't arrested Lorenzo again, have they?"

"They might as well have. It's pretty bad."

"What is? Talk to me."

Sammy tapped her shoulder. "What's going on?"

Anna mouthed her response so only Sammy could see. "Something's wrong."

Sammy leaned close to Anna, trying to hear Brooke's voice, but Michael and the captain yelling at each other must have been too loud, because she gave up and took a step back, keeping one eye on Anna, the other on the men.

"I took a call," Brooke said, "someone complaining about something they bought here. I didn't understand what he was saying at first. He was using this long Latin name."

"Like a plant name?"

"Exactly! I had to search for it online while he was griping. It turns out it's a type of mushroom, and we don't sell it. I was talking to the person when Uncle Lorenzo came in and took the phone from me."

"Is that normal?"

"No, of course not! I mean, I've gotten calls before that Uncle Lorenzo wouldn't tell me about, but I never really thought about it. I have my secrets. He has his. But now I'm worried."

Anna thought about what Brooke had said. She had to admit she didn't really understand why Brooke was so worked up. "Did Lorenzo handle it?"

"He did. He calmed the caller down, but he walked into the back room and shut the door while he was talking."

"So it sounds like everything's okay."

"While I was still on the phone, the caller threatened to call the cops on us."

"Why? You hadn't even sold him the product."

"But that's the thing. The way Uncle Lorenzo talked to him, he made it sound like we did."

"Lorenzo's selling things you don't know about? Is that the problem?"

"Not just anything, Anna. This particular mushroom is a homeopathic medicine. It's been officially categorized as a pharmaceutical by the FDA. Selling it isn't legal without a pharmaceutical license, and we don't have a license."

"Oh. Now I get it. Look, I'll be right over. Okay?" She glanced at the captain and Michael, still yelling at each other as Michael reeled in his catch. "Well, as soon as I can."

She hung up and grabbed Sammy, dragging her over to Michael and Captain Jessie, waiting until they killed the fish.

"Michael, Captain. I know we still have another hour, but is there any chance we could head back early?" She waved her phone. "I just got a call from a friend who needs me."

Captain Jessie glared at her for a moment then threw his head back and laughed. He was still laughing as he walked away with Michael's catch to pack in the cooler.

"Are you crazy?" Michael narrowed his eyes, and the red splotches on his cheeks seemed to grow. He waved toward the other passengers, laughing and chatting as they kept an eye on their rods. "Not a chance, ladies. You came out here. Now you're stuck with me."

30

Anna stared at the dark, choppy waves. "We could jump."

Sammy raised an eyebrow. "Into that?"

"The shore's not that far away," Anna said weakly, shielding her eyes as she examined the shoreline. White peaks of waves kept jumping into view. "All right, no. Of course not."

Sammy moved closer to Anna and spoke under her breath. "Look, it's not that bad. Is it? I mean, what could Michael have meant by that?"

Anna looked back over her shoulder at the other passengers. One of the fishermen raised his hand, and Anna flinched.

Just a friendly wave, she told herself. Just a friendly wave. "I'm sure it's fine. He was just being rude. Uh-oh, watch out."

The fisherman approached them, waving a beer can. His flannel shirt hung open, revealing a graying T-shirt that used to be white. A hole in the side let brown stomach hairs show through. "Ladies." He clapped one arm around Sammy while the other hand held tight to his can. His breath smelled of beer, and his fingers smelled of fish.

Sammy wrinkled her nose and wriggled out of his embrace.

"Hi," Anna said brightly. "I'm Anna McGregor. We haven't been introduced yet."

"I'm Tom, but you"—he leered at Sammy—"can call me anything you want."

Sammy shuddered and stepped farther away.

"You come out with Captain Jessie often?" Anna tried to step in between Tom and Sammy.

Tom moved to the side to keep his eyes on Sammy. "You betcha. Nothing better than catching something feisty on a morning like this, is there?"

There was no mistaking his double entendre.

"I agree. When I told my boyfriend, the cop, I was coming out, he was jealous."

Sammy's eyes widened, but she kept a straight face. "That's right," she added. "My boyfriend—the fireman—said the same thing. Too bad they had to work today, huh?"

"Cop?" Tom wrinkled his lip. "Fireman? Huh." He took a swig of beer and wiped his sleeve across his mouth. He glanced at his friend and Captain Jessie then back at the women. "All righty then. Hope you enjoy the rest of the morning."

"Creep," Sammy whispered to his retreating back. "And where was Michael while he was accosting us?"

Michael, Anna noticed, was entirely focused on his latest catch, swearing at his rod as he pulled then released the hapless fish caught on his hook. "I don't think he's going to be much help. But don't worry. We have a good sense of these guys now. As long as we keep our distance, we'll be fine. We only have to keep them away for another hour."

"I'm not afraid of those jerks. I know the type. It's all talk. He thinks we enjoy his flirting as much as he does."

"Come on, let's hold onto those rods and make sure nothing bites." Anna pulled Sammy back toward their rods. "It's still a beautiful morning, and Brooke will just have to wait."

The final hour of their trip passed slowly, but despite Captain Jessie's drinking and Tom's awkward advances, they made it back to Bluff Point Boatyard safe and sound.

As the boat pulled into the dock, Anna and Sammy were the first to jump down, leaving Captain Jessie to clean and store the rods he had loaned them. Not a nice thing to do, they knew, but they weren't likely to join another of his expeditions.

"See you later, then!" Michael called out, his annoyance clear from his voice. "I guess I'll stay and help clean up here. Don't you worry about it."

"Thanks, Michael, sorry!" Anna turned to call back to Michael with a friendly smile and a wave. "I'm just in a bit of a hurry."

She turned around and slammed right into Evan, who caught her with both hands so she didn't fall over. "Whoa. Where are you off to?"

"Evan! Hi. We're just back from our fishing trip."

"I can see that." Evan laughed. "You seem in a hurry to get away though."

"Those guys..." Sammy shook her head.

Evan's eyes opened wider, and Anna saw his jaw clench. "What happened? Did they do something?"

"No, nothing. It's fine." She tried to put his mind at ease. "They just flirted, and Sammy tends to get most of that."

Evan made a wry face. "I can imagine. Sorry you have to put up with that."

Sammy shrugged. "Thanks. I'm used to it. But do you mind if we take off?"

"Of course, sorry to keep you." Evan looked back at the boat. "I'm going to be here for a while. I've got some more questions for your friend Michael."

Anna gave his hand a quick squeeze, then she and Sammy hurried away from the marina and the watching men. They kept their pace all the way back to town and, within ten minutes, were calling out a greeting to Brooke as they entered the Magic Shop.

"Anna, Sammy. Thank you for coming."

"I'm just sorry we couldn't get here faster. We were out on a boat. There was nothing we could do."

"That's okay." Brooke raised both hands. "Don't worry. Nothing's happened in the meantime. Uncle Lorenzo is off doing one of his magic shows, so it's just me here."

"Okay," Anna said, "now tell me everything again."

As Brooke reviewed her mysterious phone conversation, she, Anna, and Sammy walked up and down the aisles, looking for anything that might be mistaken for the illegal drug the stranger had accused Lorenzo of selling. Nothing in the front of the shop fit the description, so they turned their attention to the back room.

Cardboard boxes stood stacked in piles of four or five, each clearly labeled with black marker. Anna saw boxes of puzzles, toys, magic tricks, books. Other boxes held figurines, hats, and T-shirts. It seemed like they had even more products available back there than were displayed in the front of the shop.

"It's a small shop," Brooke explained. "We don't have space to display everything, but we know what's back here, so if someone asks for something, I can come back and find it."

"You have food items back here too?" Sammy asked, amazed. "Is that safe?"

Brooke picked up a sealed plastic bag stored with other similar bags in a large crate. "These are all dried. We don't sell anything fresh, so it's not a problem."

"Hm." Sammy didn't sound convinced.

"What's through here?" Anna pulled open a heavy metal door at the back of the room. The door opened onto a small courtyard walled in on every side. Despite the high walls surrounding it, the midday sun exposed every corner of the space, which was neat and tidy. Along one wall, someone had stacked plastic chairs next to a folding table and a potting bench, which was wiped clean. Rows of flower beds filled half the space, each bed neatly bounded by bricks and clearly labeled. At least, the labels were there. Anna couldn't actually read any of them. She examined each of the plants.

"That's not marijuana, is it?" She pointed at one of the plants.

"Why are you asking me?" Sammy asked with a laugh.

"It's not," Brooke answered. "I know because I asked Uncle Lorenzo that before."

"Hm." Anna wasn't sure she could trust Lorenzo's denial. "I don't recognize most of these plants. He's got a pretty eclectic garden here."

Brooke rubbed her hands along her arms. "Come on. We better get back inside in case a customer comes."

They paused in the back room as Anna took one more look around. She wasn't really sure what she was looking for, but if Brooke was right, Lorenzo was engaged in some kind of illegal sales, and Anna needed to find out what—and if it was connected to Oliver's murder.

"What are you ladies looking for? Can I help?"

None of them had heard Lorenzo come in, and they all jumped. Anna swallowed, not sure how to explain why she was searching Lorenzo's private space.

31

Brooke spoke up, approaching her uncle and placing her hand on his arm. "Uncle Lorenzo, I'm worried. What are you selling that someone wants to call the police on you? Is this connected to that murder?"

"What? Murder?" Lorenzo's bushy eyebrows shot up. "No, of course not. Don't worry, darling. It's nothing."

Anna's gaze fell on another bag of dried flowers, but these she recognized. She picked up the bag. "These flowers, are they for a home remedy?"

"Uncle! You're doing that again?"

Lorenzo pushed Brook's hand off his arm, strode over to Anna, and snatched the bag from her. "That's none of your business. Look." He took a breath, and Anna realized she'd been holding hers. "Brooke, darling, it's not a con, and I'm not practicing medicine. But people who live near here rely on things like this. I'm selling them something they need. What's wrong with that?"

"It's true. That is a useful herb," Anna agreed. "I know. I ran into some of the home remedies used in the communities where I did my research. A lot of Hispanic and Latino communities use it in this part of the state."

Lorenzo opened his arms wide. "So you know, it is completely innocent."

"Then why isn't it on your shelves out front?" Sammy asked.

"Well... bah—" Lorenzo stumbled over his words then waved one hand and stomped back out to the front room.

"Brooke, you should know that Lorenzo is breaking the law by selling some of these things, even though they're generally safe," Anna said. "I should have recognized this sooner. Look." She led the group back out to the garden, walking up and down the rows of plants until she saw what she was looking for. "There. See? The pointy leaves, green with a chalky whiteness to them." She pulled out her phone and did a quick internet search. Once she found what she was looking for, she held up her phone to show Brooke and Sammy the picture of the same plant growing in the garden. "Lorenzo is selling estafiate."

Sammy looked closer at the image on the phone. "This says it's artemisia."

"That's the scientific name. Estafiate is the common name. You might also have heard it called cudweed, sagewort, or silver sagebrush."

"Great." Brooke leaned heavily against the folded table, her head drooping. "So this probably needs a license to sell, too, right?"

Anna shook her head. "Not this one. It's not categorized as a pharmaceutical."

"How is it used?"

"The leaves and flowers are steeped in boiling water to make a tea to treat various ailments like stomachaches and fever. Some people use it to treat rheumatism, thanks to its supposedly anti-inflammatory properties."

Brooke perked up. "That doesn't sound bad. And you said people appreciate having it."

"They do. It's true. But they need to be careful, and so does Lorenzo."

"Why?"

"There are a lot of species and varieties of this plants. And it's very closely related to wormwood."

"Wormwood!" Sammy jumped in. "I've heard of that. It's a poison. Isn't it?"

Brooke nodded. "I remember reading about that."

"That's right," Anna said. "Estafiate seems to be safer than wormwood, at least as a tea for adults, but unfortunately, there are no clinical trials to ensure the correct dosage or its safety. In any case, we just don't know enough about the safety of long-term use. Estafiate contains some chemical compounds that could be toxic to the nervous system in certain forms."

"I know my uncle," Brooke said. "He's only selling it because he knows people want it and it can help. It's the same reason he sells the other herbs and tools for witchcraft."

"He believes in witchcraft?" Sammy asked.

"Well... no... I guess not. But he does believe in spirits. He's very spiritual."

"Like séances and things like that?"

Brooke laughed. "I don't think he'd go that far. He may believe in the spirits, but he also believes they can't be controlled, can't be asked for favors."

"But he sells things that people use to do just that," Anna pointed out.

Brooke shrugged. "Is it a con if you sell things you don't believe in but other people think will help?"

Sammy barked out a laugh. "Ha, if so, every store selling face cream would be indicted."

Laughing, Brooke went to calm down her uncle, then the three women headed toward the community center to pick up Eoin.

"You sounded so calm back there, talking about these magical herbs," Sammy said. "You don't believe in witchcraft, do you?"

"They're not magical." Anna laughed. "They're just known to have certain medicinal properties. It's not magic, and no, I don't believe in magic or witchcraft or ghosts." They walked along in silence for a minute before Anna continued. "But I am worried about Lorenzo. He has an awful lot of secrets."

"He does seem to like skirting the law, doesn't he?" Sammy agreed.

"Oh, I don't know about that." Brooke offered a half-hearted defense for her uncle. "I mean, nothing dangerous. He's an active member of the small business association in town, and no one there's complained."

"I know the woman who runs that, Angela Nelson. She's a straight shooter. You'd know if she had any problems. On the other hand, Oliver has a reputation as someone who's likely to report any activity he considers suspect," Anna pointed out.

"Would he consider witchcraft and medicinal herbs suspect?" Sammy asked.

"Oh my!"

Mrs. Santiago's exclamation brought Anna and Sammy up short.

"Mrs. Santiago, Mrs. James," Anna greeted them. "Sorry, I didn't see you."

Mrs. James shook her head. "No, you were too busy talking about magic and witchcraft."

Mrs. Santiago made a distinct tutting sound. "Good afternoon, ladies."

Anna looked up to see they were approaching the church on Washington Mall. "Are you both coming from the church?" She smiled.

"We are." Mrs. James's mouth pulled tight in disapproval as she talked. "It was too bad we didn't see you there, Anna, Brooke, and... your friend."

"Right, sorry." Anna introduced the older women to Sammy, who smiled warmly and shook their hands, offering compliments on their dresses and hair. Anna rolled her eyes. She didn't mean to do it, but somehow Sammy managed to make everyone like her.

"You were talking about Lorenzo," Mrs. Santiago said. "I know he's your uncle, Brooke, and family is important, but I don't trust him."

"I don't either." Mrs. James nodded vigorously. "After all, he deals in witchcraft and wizardry."

"That's a little harsh." Anna put an arm around Brooke. "He's a magician! He does children's parties."

"There is that story about the fight," Mrs. James said.

"What fight?" Anna asked.

"Really?" Sammy asked.

"Oh yes." Mrs. James warmed to her topic. "He'd just moved here. You may not remember this, Brooke. You were helping your parents with their move."

"Some teenage boys were causing trouble," Mrs. Santiago added.

"Yes. Lorenzo took matters into his own hands," Mrs. James continued.

"That doesn't sound like a fight," Anna pointed out.

"No? He was very violent. He rounded them up. He hit them."

"What?"

Mrs. James's head bobbed up and down. "He smacked them."

"Got them together and dragged them out into his car," Mrs. Santiago finished the story.

"Where did he take them?"

"Who knows?"

Brooke's laughter broke the tense mood. "Ladies, calm down. I know the story perfectly well. He took them back to their parents. I do remember that. The town should be thanking him for that, not gossiping about it."

"Well." Mrs. James sniffed and adjusted her sleeve. "He should have left that to the police."

Brooke put her hands on her hips. "He was angry, and he was trying to help."

"Anger never helps, dear."

"Lovely to see you ladies, as always." Anna grabbed Brooke and dragged her away before she got angry herself. That wouldn't do anyone any good. She was trying to prove Lorenzo's innocence, and that should not include turning the town against Brooke and her uncle.

"Come on, we need to get to the community center before Eoin causes any trouble." She glanced at her watch. "BethAnne dropped him at a class this morning after breakfast, and it ended about five minutes ago."

Sammy tucked her arm into Anna's, and they picked up their pace.

"I'm just so grateful you believe me," Brooke said, panting a bit—whether from anger or walking fast, Anna wasn't sure. "How can those horrid ladies say those things about Uncle Lorenzo?"

"I know, honey. I'm sorry. Gossip hurts so many people."

Anna grabbed Brooke's arm as well, and the three of them marched on, spanning the sidewalk. They laughed as they walked, letting the activity raise their spirits. They were still laughing as they swung around a corner—and walked directly into Steve and Coral.

"Anna!"

"Steve." Anna shifted her gave to the woman. "Coral."

"Anna." Coral smirked.

"Now that that's over," Sammy chimed in, "sorry we can't stop to chat. We must be going."

This time, it was Anna's turn to be dragged away by Sammy and Brooke, which Anna knew was for the best. Just seeing Steve with that woman made her anger rise. She let her friends pull her along, knowing that Mrs. James was absolutely right. Anger never helped.

32

Anna found it impossible to be angry for long with Eoin trotting along next to her, chatting away. The exhibit at the convention center had hundreds of photographs and all kinds of stories about people who'd lived there and people who'd died there. He asked if she knew how many famous people had stayed in Cape May and that they had old photographs of Climbing Rose Cottage.

She tried to keep track of everything he told her but eventually realized she just needed to listen with an occasional "Oh!" or "I see." She loved how excited Eoin was to learn about Cape May. This was a summer he would never forget, for sure. Though she supposed last month's murder had kind of settled that already.

A honk from a passing jeep brought her attention back to the street in front of them. They'd stopped at an intersection to wait for the light to change before crossing. A well-muscled arm waved as the jeep pulled over on the street ahead of them.

Anna leaned into the side window. Eoin stood on tiptoe

but still could only get the top of his head to the level of the window.

"Luke, you're towing your boat. Does that mean it's water ready?" Anna asked.

"Might be." Luke tapped lightly on his steering wheel. "I'm taking her down to the marina now to give her a quick test."

Anna stepped back to examine the boat again. "It really looks beautiful. That's not surprising, knowing the carpenter who worked on it."

"You built that?" Eoin's awe carried in his voice and in his wide eyes.

Luke turned in his seat to look back at the boat. "I didn't build her from nothing, but I rebuilt her. She was in pretty dire straits when I got ahold of her."

Eoin walked the length of the boat, running his hand along the smooth side. Once he reached the front of the jeep again, he pulled out his notebook and pen.

"I still have some more work to do on her," Luke said. "But I can do that at the marina."

"Which marina do you use?" Anna pictured the fancy boats she'd seen at the Cape May Marina. Luke had done a great job fixing his boat up, but it would stick out like a sore thumb among those opulent floating mansions.

"Bluff Point Boatyard," Luke answered, putting her mind at ease. "Most of the locals use it. The other marinas tend to cater to folks who need a place to store their boats but only come down a few times a year to use them."

"Sure, I know it."

"You do?" Luke raised his eyebrows in surprise. "I didn't know you were a boat person."

"I'm not." Anna shook her head. "I went fishing this morning with a friend, and that's where we departed from. Come to think of it"—she rubbed a finger over her chin—"I think that's where Detective Walsh keeps his boat too."

"Oh, great." Luke groaned. "I hope I don't see him there now."

"Well, you might not see him, but you probably will see Evan. He was there when we got back from our fishing trip less than an hour ago. He was questioning people about the murder."

Michael was probably still there too. He'd offered to stay behind and help wash down the boat after their trip. She wondered if Evan would question him as well. She hoped so.

"I'm glad I ran into you," Luke said. "Want to grab lunch later? It won't take me long to get her settled in." He gestured toward his boat with his thumb. "I could take you out somewhere."

"Not today." Anna gave the boat one more look. "I'm having lunch with Evan, but thanks. Maybe another time."

Luke's brows lowered. "Lunch with Evan, huh? Isn't he supposed to be busy solving a murder or something?"

Anna laughed then stopped when she realized Luke wasn't laughing. "Right. Of course. But he does need to eat."

"Yeah, sure. Don't we all?" Luke gunned his engine and pulled away from the curb a little faster than he should have given the size of the load he was hauling.

"That was abrupt," Anna said to herself as much as to Eoin.

Eoin looked up at her, his forehead wrinkled. "He was angry."

"Why?" Anna meant the question to be rhetorical. If she didn't know why Luke was angry, she didn't expect Eoin to.

"He's jealous, isn't he?" Eoin answered.

Anna glared at him. "That can't be it."

Eoin shrugged. "I'm telling you what I saw. He's jealous because you're having lunch with Evan instead of him."

"Hmm." Anna bit her lip. "Come on." She wrapped an arm around Eoin and hugged him close. "I'm sorry you had to see that. And it's not just me having lunch with Evan. You're joining us too."

Eoin's eyes lit up, knowing he would get to spend time with his hero.

33

"This is a perfect picnic lunch, Evan," Anna said then covered her mouth as she yawned.

"So perfect it's putting you to sleep?" Evan replied with surprise.

"No, sorry." Anna waved away the thought. "Not at all. I'm so sorry. This really is gorgeous."

Eoin, his mouth stuffed with pepperoni, nodded enthusiastically.

The spread really was tremendous. Evan had brought fresh Italian bread, three different cheeses, pickles, pepperoni, salami, plum tomatoes, bean salad—everything Anna could possibly want—and he'd carried it all in a classic picnic basket covered with a red-and-white-checked napkin. He'd even been thoughtful enough to bring special treats for Tough Cookie, who had joined them on the front porch.

"So why the yawn? Didn't you sleep well last night?"

"I slept fine, just not long enough. Sammy and I met Michael at five o'clock this morning."

"Ah, right. The fishing trip. I hope you were able to enjoy it, despite the unwanted attention."

Anna finished chewing her bread and cheese as she thought about it. They'd only gone a mile or so offshore, just far enough to enjoy the cool ocean breeze but still see the picturesque houses of Cape May. The sun had been bright but not too hot. The captain had been quiet but generally polite. Despite a few scares about Michael's temper and Tom's flirting, it had been a good experience. But that wasn't really why she'd gone.

"It was a gorgeous morning to be out on a boat," she finally answered.

"Catch anything?" Evan's grin made it clear he expected the answer to be no.

"No." Anna threw a napkin at Evan, who caught it before it hit his face. "Michael caught a few flukes."

"Summer flounder." Evan nodded. "Sounds like you had fun." He toyed with his glass of lemonade.

Anna felt another yawn coming on and bent her head down to hide it. As tired as she was, and as disappointed that her early-morning adventure hadn't revealed anything significant about Michael or Brad or Oliver, it had been exhilarating. She could still feel the sun and wind on her face. She looked up to find Evan watching her closely.

"You okay?" he asked.

"Of course." She laughed. "Just thinking about how pleasant it was out on the boat this morning."

"So, why did you decide to go out with that guy Michael? You barely know him."

"Oh. Um." Anna felt Eoin's eyes on her and knew she couldn't lie. "Well, to tell the truth..."

"Don't tell me," Evan said as Anna trailed off. "You're trying to investigate the latest murder. Aren't you?"

Anna shrugged and gave Evan her most innocent look.

It might have worked if Eoin hadn't chimed in. "I've been taking notes." He pulled out his notebook after carefully wiping his hands off on his shorts.

Anna glowered at him and pointed at his napkin.

"See? Cousin Anna's friend Steve wants to help. Ms. Brooke and her uncle don't want to be involved. And Mr. and Mrs. Ahava think there might be a ghost." Eoin looked up at Evan, his expression serious. "I saw old photographs, y'know. Cape May might really have ghosts."

"That's quite a list you have there, young man. May I see it?" Evan held out a hand, and Eoin tentatively passed him the notebook. He clearly didn't want to give it away.

Evan flipped through a few pages then gave it back. Eoin's shoulders relaxed noticeably once he had it back in his pocket. "Now, why are you writing down things like that?"

Eoin shrugged. "I just write down what I hear. That's all."

"This is your doing. Isn't it?" Evan wagged a finger at Anna. "You're asking questions about murder again."

"Maybe I am." Anna lowered her brows. "Instead of just telling me off, talk to me. How is your investigation going?"

Evan rolled his eyes and shook his head, but Anna stared him down. Finally, he said, "Look, we have a few suspects but nothing definitive. It's still early. At this point, we're looking at everything about the crime—where he was killed, who was around at the time of the murder, and who might have motive."

"This would have been Thursday night, right?" Anna asked.

Evan nodded. "His body was found early Friday morning, so he was in the water for a while. We're pretty sure he was dropped off a boat somewhere in Spicer Creek."

"But so many boats pass through there," Anna pointed out. "Surely someone would have seen something."

"It depends when it happened," Evan said. "We still need to talk to that boy, David, to find out what he heard and if it's relevant. His parents have been hard to tie down. Assuming the killer strangled Oliver inside the boat's cabin, it would just be a matter of sliding him overboard. He'd be heavy, but a strong man could do it without making too much noise."

Anna thought about that. A strong man. Lorenzo was a big man, no question. Then again, so was everyone else involved in this.

"Luke is still on our radar," Evan said softly. "I know he's your friend."

"Luke? No way." Anna laughed off the suggestion. She knew Luke wasn't a killer. Though he had been kind of upset when she saw him before lunch. And he did have a boat.

Eoin crawled forward to whisper in Anna's ear. "Don't forget how jealous he was."

Despite his best effort, Eoin's whisper carried, and Anna was sure Evan heard.

If he had, he didn't say. "He's your friend, so you probably already know he has a temper."

"How about Brad Atherton? He has a boat at the Cape May Marina."

"And an alibi," Evan replied. "He had dinner that night with a group of people. They were together at the restaurant then back at his boat as well."

"So his alibi puts him in the right place?" Eoin asked.

Evan leaned over and ruffled Eoin's red hair. The boy frowned and ran his own hand through it, though it was just as messy as before Evan touched it.

"Yes, but he wasn't alone. Either everyone who had

dinner with him is in on it..." He held up a hand when Anna opened her mouth. "Or he didn't do it."

"Maybe they are all in on it!" she exclaimed. "Maybe it's a conspiracy."

Evan rolled his eyes again.

They'll get stuck that way if he keeps it up, she thought. "Okay, I guess that's not the most likely scenario." She watched Tough Cookie chase a critter through the flower bed, then turned her eyes toward Evan. "And what about Steve? Did he tell you he was at the conference in Philly? Because he wasn't."

"I can't tell you what Steve told me. You know that," Evan said. When Anna glared at him, he added. "But if it makes you feel better, he doesn't have an alibi, and he's not off our suspect list."

"Ha!" She laughed then realized it didn't really make her feel better. "So I guess Brad's dinner party is Michael's alibi too?"

Evan nodded. "Yep. I checked it out. They all confirm they had dinner at the Red Tavern, then they went to Brad's boat for drinks. He must have a pretty fancy setup there."

"He does. Believe me."

Evan looked surprised. "You were on his boat?"

Anna blushed. "I met Michael there on Sunday." She didn't think it was necessary to include the part about her snooping around the docks. "So the dinner went all night?"

"Yep, dinner then drinks on his boat. They all confirm it, and they drove over together. Well, it looks like Michael drove."

"That doesn't surprise me."

"Michael says he didn't even know Oliver was in town. He's surprised. Oliver usually calls when he's coming down.

Oliver knew about Brad's boat." Evan took a deep breath. "Lorenzo has no alibi."

"No, not Lorenzo. Uh-huh." Anna shook her head. "What about that guy who works at the yacht club? Dennis."

Evan started packing up what was left of their meal. "We talked to him, of course, but he's not really a suspect. Nothing indicates he knew the victim."

"Hm." Anna grabbed the last piece of Manchego before Evan packed it up. "He should be a suspect. He's suspicious. That's for sure."

Evan laughed. "That's not the same thing, and you know it."

With the remaining food neatly stored in the basket, Evan leaned back, his face turned to the sun. Anna watched him, the way the sun reflected the red highlights in his hair, ruffled slightly by the wind.

"I guess I should be getting back." Evan sat up with a start. "We hope to talk to David and his parents this evening, when they're both home from work."

"Hello there!"

Anna looked up at the sound of the saccharine voice. Oh, fudge. Her two least favorite people in the world, Steve and Coral, stood outside her gate.

❈ 34 ❈

"Hello!" Coral called again, as if anyone could have missed the first high-pitched squeal. She flapped her hand in a motion that was probably some type of wave and smiled broadly.

Anna felt herself tense. Oh no, now what?

Steve's hand on Coral's back left an impression in her blouse that suggested he was trying to encourage the woman to keep walking, but to no avail. With Coral's second call, she pushed the gate open and approached the porch, still flapping her hand.

"Oh good, Coral," Evan said in a flat voice. Apparently the woman had made as good an impression on him as she had on Anna. Evan took yet another step up in Anna's estimation.

Pursing her lips and creasing her forehead, Anna blinked and tried to think of something positive. "I'm glad we had the chance to talk." She touched Evan's shoulder.

"Me too." He smiled down at her. "And like I said, we'll be talking with David and his folks this evening, so we'll find out what his story is and if it's connected to the murder."

"Ooh, talking about the murder?" Coral had closed the distance from the front gate despite Steve's clear reluctance.

"And, Anna," Evan said before acknowledging Coral, "make sure to thank BethAnne for me, for doing the right thing and getting David to talk about what he heard."

Anna grinned when she saw the creases run across Coral's lips. "Of course." She turned to face Coral and Steve. "Good afternoon. How are you both?"

"Well, aren't you formal, dear?" Coral laughed and swatted at Anna with a hand. "Patrolman Burley, how are *you* doing? Do remind me, when is the next Environmental Commission meeting?"

"Oh, um," Evan stumbled over his words, surprised by the question. "I'm not really sure."

"Steve, darling." Coral grabbed Steve's hand. "I may not have told you, but I'm involved in a number of commissions in town. I was appointed by the mayor, you see. Patrolman Burley—Evan," she smirked at Evan as she said his name, "represents the police department for these commissions."

"Low man on the totem pole, eh?" Steve laughed.

Evan started to laugh as well then saw the look in Coral's eyes. "Right. Um, sure. I'm just going to get these things washed up." He grabbed the basket and threw the remaining plates and napkins into it, then headed into the house.

"Anna, you've done wonders with this property." Coral glanced around as she spoke. "It looks so much better now than the wreck it was when your great-aunt Louise was alive. Just a little more work, and it will be beautiful."

Anna coughed to hide her amazement at Coral's rudeness. She really shouldn't be surprised. "Yes, I've done a lot of work on it. It's important to me." She spoke clearly, hoping to get Coral to realize that her words could be interpreted as rude.

"Oh, look," Coral continued, "you have hostas in your garden. How quaint." She bent down to run her hands along the tall flowers shooting up from the hostas then jumped back with a cry. "Ew! What is that? A black rat?"

"What? Where?" Anna ran down the steps to see what Coral was talking about then laughed. "Coral, that's my cat, Tough Cookie."

"Oh, a cat. How... um, cute."

"Right." Even Tough Cookie looked like she didn't believe that one. She glared at Coral with pure disdain, rubbed against her leg, leaving a trail of black and white hair along her peach trousers, and stalked away.

"Oh." Coral focused on rubbing the hair off her pants.

"I'm very lucky to have met up with Coral," Steve said.

Anna jumped, not realizing he had approached so close behind her.

"Yes. I didn't realize you knew each other." Anna couldn't imagine he'd have had a connection in Cape May she didn't know about. Then again, he'd been doing a lot of things she didn't know about.

"We didn't," Coral cooed, not yet done with her trousers but apparently not willing to let Anna have a private conversation with Steve. "But when I saw this beautiful young man, I could have sworn I recognized him."

Beautiful? Anna couldn't hide her smile as she looked at Steve, who slowly turned red.

"Right. Um," Steve mumbled. "Turns out I was at Coral's brother's wedding in Philadelphia."

"Whose wedding?" Anna tried to remember the event. "Was I there?"

Steve hemmed and hawed. "Um, no, I don't think you were. We were keeping... well, you know... people didn't know..."

"Right. So you didn't invite me to keep our relationship secret." Anna's anger rose. He might have even mentioned it to her. She'd been so in love with him, she'd agreed completely to keeping their relationship secret. What a fool she'd been, a blind fool.

Evan came out of the house, the empty basket on his arm. "It was good to see you both. I have to get back to work." He smiled down at Anna, and she knew without a doubt that what she'd told Michael was true—she was defi-nitely happier.

She took Evan's hand. "I'll see you soon, right?"

Evan looked almost as surprised as Steve did at her gesture, but Coral looked furious.

"Don't forget, Steve, Detective Walsh will want to interview you still," Evan said.

"He will?" Anna asked.

Evan lowered his brows at her. "Police business, Anna. You know that."

Anna blushed. Coral grinned. Tough Cookie took the opportunity to rub against Coral's leg one more time.

✿ 35 ✿

"Hi, Felicia," Anna whispered, leaning over the reference desk. "How are things going?" She glanced back to see Eoin already sitting cross-legged on the floor in front of his favorite bookshelf, the one that held histories of Cape May. *No accounting for tastes*, she thought but smiled at the sight.

"Anna, what brings you and Eoin around?" Felicia asked as she finished checking out a patron.

"We're hoping to see BethAnne. Her school ended an hour ago. She should be here by now, right?"

"Oh, yes." Felicia looked at the clock on the wall. "I haven't seen her yet. But, Anna, I'm glad you're here. I have some information that might interest you." Felicia's eyes twinkled.

Anna laughed then slapped her hand over her mouth. "Felicia, you're really getting into this detective thing. Aren't you? If I didn't know better, I'd say you were enjoying it."

Felicia blushed and looked away.

"I'm sorry. I shouldn't tease you. What have you learned?"

In response to Anna's teasing, Felicia took the time to straighten some books on the counter in front of her before responding, but finally, she raised one eyebrow. "Kathy learned it, actually, and it's about that fellow Brad you were asking about."

"Brad Atherton?" Anna asked. "Great."

"It seems his family doesn't have the happy home life his parents try to portray. They're both quite well-known in certain circles, you see."

"I read about that. His father is a local politician, right? And his mother is some kind of socialite."

"That's right," Felicia replied. "Well, publicly, they talk about how important family is, having a structured life, that sort of thing." She rolled her eyes as she spoke. "Of course, we all know what that means."

Anna nodded. "I do. So that's their public stance. What about their private stance? Any affairs with the pool boy or something like that?"

Felicia giggled. "Not quite. It turns out there was a family split. One of the boys, Brad's brother, was disowned, completely kicked out of the family, out of the will, every-thing. The parents don't even talk about him anymore. They pretend he doesn't exist."

"That's terrible," Anna said with feeling. "I did hear about that. Michael Chan told me Brad's father disowned his brother because he'd failed out of school and embar-rassed him. As if embarrassing his father is the only thing that matters in the world."

"Oh, you knew?" Felicia's expression dropped. "Kathy wanted me to tell you. She thought it might be significant."

Anna reached out to pat Felicia's arm. "Thank you. I appreciate her passing that on, and please tell her so. If she knows, then that means it's not quite the secret Brad and Michael seem to think."

"How anyone would think they could keep that kind of family gossip out of the public eye..." Felicia shook her head.

Anna looked back up at the clock then glanced around the library. "Still no BethAnne?"

"Oh." Felicia frowned. "She really should be here by now. Perhaps she had something else to do after school today."

A phone rang in the office behind Felicia, who excused herself to answer it.

Anna turned her back on the desk and watched Eoin. The boy was absorbed in the book he held open on his lap, oblivious to people passing by him. Every few minutes, however, he rose and looked around the library, standing on his toes to peer over the shelves. Looking for Beth-Anne, no doubt. Anna knew how much that girl meant to Eoin.

"Anna."

Anna spun around at the tension in Felicia's voice. Felicia's brow was furrowed, and she twisted her hands together.

"What's wrong? What happened?"

"That was BethAnne's mother. She's looking for Beth-Anne, too. She's called everyone she can think of. She's getting worried."

Anna inhaled sharply. She didn't want to panic. She certainly didn't want to scare Eoin. But BethAnne wasn't where she was supposed to be, and her mother didn't even know where she was. She was just a child—a precocious one, certainly, but still just a child. And she'd been missing for over an hour.

"We need to call the police," she said.

"Her mother is doing that now. She wanted to check with me before she did."

Anna nodded. "That makes sense. Where else could she be?" She looked back at Eoin.

As soon as he saw her expression, he jumped up and ran to her. "Cousin Anna, what's wrong?"

"We're just not sure where BethAnne is, honey, but you don't need to worry." Anna tried to keep her voice light. "Come on. Let's go look for her."

36

As Anna thought furiously about where else she could look for BethAnne, she realized with dismay just how little she really knew about the girl. She knew BethAnne loved the library, loved reading and learning. Maybe she was still at school? Maybe the debate team had called a sudden meeting, and BethAnne hadn't let her mother know?

Anna took Eoin's hand, and together, they speed-walked to the local high school. As they approached the building, two police cars pulled up in front. Anna didn't recognize the uniformed officers who walked into the school but was relieved to see them.

Okay, no point in duplicating their efforts.

"What do you know about BethAnne, Eoin?" she asked her cousin. "Where else might she be?"

Eoin screwed up his face with the effort of his thoughts. "The library... the school... her house..." He ticked the places off on his fingers as he said them. Then his eyes brightened. "David's house? They like to play video games at David's house. His system is better than hers," he added knowingly.

"Of course, David. Come on."

Even as they trotted along, Anna realized the police would certainly have thought of David too. He had reached out to them, after all. So she was not surprised to see yet another police car parked in front of the house Eoin identified as David's. As they stood on the sidewalk, deciding what to do, Evan came out of the house.

"Anna, Eoin." His face was grim, his voice serious. "I'm glad you're both okay. We have officers all over town looking for the teenagers."

"I'm so glad to hear it." Anna tightened her grip on Eoin's hand then gasped. "Did you say teenagers? Plural?"

Evan nodded. "Both BethAnne and David are missing. It hasn't been long, only a couple of hours now, so we have to hope for the best." He paused, looking down at Eoin. "Don't get too worried, little man."

Eoin nodded seriously, but Anna felt his hand trembling. He was as worried about BethAnne and David as she was, maybe even more.

As they stood watching Evan drive off to continue the search, Anna's phone rang. She snatched it up. "BethAnne?" she asked without waiting for the other person to speak.

"Oh. No, I'm sorry. Anna? Is that you? Lorenzo Cortinas here."

"Oh, Lorenzo. I'm sorry, I didn't mean... I mean, hi."

"Is this a bad time?" he asked.

"Kind of, yes. Do you need something?"

"If you're busy, perhaps not. I shouldn't have bothered you."

Anna bit her lip. She was being rude. "Please, not at all.

I'm glad you called, and I'm happy to talk. What's on your mind?"

"I have a feeling..." The man paused dramatically, and Anna took a breath, trying not to let her impatience come through the phone.

"What kind of feeling?"

"To be honest, Anna, I'm worried. Something isn't right here."

"Where? Are you at the shop?"

"No, I'm at the marina. Bluff Point Boatyard. I'm working a magic show."

Eoin tugged on her arm, and she looked down to see his eyes wide, his face red. "Anna, we have to find BethAnne."

"I know, Eoin. I'll be done in a second."

"Did I hear you're looking for someone? Is someone missing?" Lorenzo asked.

"Yes, two teenagers."

"Anna, something is wrong here. I don't know what. It's just a feeling. But I wanted to let you know that something doesn't feel right. Here. At the marina. You've been so interested in the murder, and I don't know if this is connected, but..."

"Can you give me a clue what's wrong?" Anna asked with frustration.

"I can't be specific. I'm very sorry. It's a feeling. Call it a premonition."

Anna looked down at Eoin. She couldn't respond to Lorenzo's premonition. It could be nothing, and it could distract her from finding BethAnne.

"Cousin Anna." Eoin tugged at her sleeve again. "Mr. Cortinas had a premonition?"

Anna nodded, covering the phone with her hand. "Yes. Why?"

Eoin pulled out his notebook. "It could be important. Look. It can't be a coincidence."

"What do you mean?"

"Anna, are you still there?" Lorenzo's voice reminded her she was still on the phone.

"Yes, sorry. Look, Lorenzo, I'll come down as soon as I can, okay? But I'm not sure when."

"I understand. You can't go running around, chasing old men's premonitions." The phone disconnected.

"It's not a premonition, Cousin Anna," Eoin almost shouted. "Or a feeling. It must be something he saw, but he doesn't realize he saw it."

Anna gaped at Eoin. "Why would you say that?"

Just then, her phone rang again. This time, she saw who was calling. "Evan, any news?"

"Nothing new. I just didn't want to talk in front of Eoin or upset him."

Anna looked down at the boy still waving his notebook in the air. "Good thinking. What's going on?"

"We have officers from neighboring towns helping with the search. The kids have only been missing for two hours, so it's too early to panic. But with children, we take this seriously. I know I said we could assume the best, but for our investigation, we're assuming the worst. We have people searching the beaches, the canal, anywhere the kids could have gotten hurt or into trouble."

Anna bit her lip and tried to keep a smile on her face. "Thanks for letting me know. It's good to know that you all are taking this so seriously."

"Absolutely. The department has also requested support from the State Police, since they have tools we don't have. Once they're involved, they can expand the search, locate the kids' cell phones, things like that."

Anna let out a breath. She knew what she was about to

say would sound foolish, but she didn't have any better ideas. "I think we might head to the marina."

"The marina? Why?" Evan asked.

"Lorenzo has a feeling," she replied, her voice flat.

"Uh-huh."

"But Eoin thinks it's more than a feeling."

"More than a feeling? Are you channeling song lyrics?"

"Ugh!"

Eoin waved his notebook in front of her face. "It's all in here, Cousin Anna. Lorenzo notices things. He's got keen eyes. That's how he survived as a con man."

"A what?" Evan asked.

"Nothing, nothing." Anna covered the phone. "He's not a con man, Eoin."

Eoin gave her a look of disdain.

How did an eight-year-old make her feel naïve? "Right. Gotcha." She uncovered the phone. "Evan, Eoin has a point. We're heading over there now."

37

Bluff Point Boatyard was busier than it had been on Monday morning. This afternoon, the pool area was packed. All the folding chairs were occupied, either by people or towels, and groups of youngsters and adults gathered in pockets throughout the pool. Beyond the main pool, Anna could see the splash pool for the little kids, then beyond that, the tiki bar for their exhausted parents.

Lorenzo stood at the edge of the parking lot, just beyond the concrete pad surrounding the pool. As soon as he saw them, he waved his arms to flag them down.

A completely unnecessary move on his part. They could hardly miss him.

"Lorenzo, hi. Now tell me again, what's bugging you?"

"Like I told you, and Brooke knows, sometimes I sense things." He looked across the parking lot to the marina on the far side as he spoke, Cape May Marina. "Something is definitely not right there." He grabbed Anna by the elbow and led her to the side of the parking lot closer to the pool, away from the Cape May Marina.

She took Eoin's hand, and the three of them traipsed into the chaos.

Anna peered back around at the other marina, looking for anything that struck her as odd or not belonging. "Did you see something specific that made you feel off?"

Eoin leaned around Anna to see then jumped back as water cascaded toward him from a large boy's cannonball. He pushed his notebook back into the security of his dry pocket.

When Lorenzo just shrugged, Anna said, "Okay, let's walk through it. What did you do when you got here? Did you know something was wrong right off the bat?"

"No." Lorenzo frowned and ran his fingers along his chin. "No, I came in, set up, and got right to work with my tricks."

Eoin braved the risk of getting wet to walk along the edge of the pool. He stayed on his toes, jumping out of the way whenever necessary but soaking up everything he saw.

"And what tricks did you do?" Anna asked, keeping one eye on Eoin.

"Ah, well, my usual routine. You know the stuff, float-ing... moving through glass... just the usual."

Anna raised an eyebrow. "Usual? Huh. Okay then, did all the tricks go the way they were supposed to? Did your audience enjoy them?"

"Of course, I always do well." Lorenzo didn't sound arrogant. He was just a magician who was sure of his routine. Then he frowned. "I started worrying while I was doing my balloon tricks."

"Why?" She glanced down to see that Eoin had tucked himself safely behind her again to write down everything Lorenzo said.

Lorenzo snapped his fingers. "That's it. As I inflated a balloon, I remembered something I saw when I went to the shed to get my air pump." Lorenzo waved toward a gray wooden shed in the far corner of the parking lot, closer to the other marina. "I keep my air pump in there. This is the only place I use it, and I don't like to carry it around. But while I was there, I saw something."

"So is that what got you worried?" Anna trotted across the lot to the shed, Eoin close on her heels. She stood facing the shed, hands on her hips. She looked for anything suspicious on the shed itself then turned slightly to look around the parking lot, back at Bluff Point Boatyard, then across to the much quieter Cape May Marina. Standing silently, she heard masts clanging even over the screeches of playing children carrying from the pool.

Lorenzo looked around as well, then at Anna, then back toward the Cape May Marina. "It was something there. That's what made me feel like something was wrong."

She had no idea if it was connected to BethAnne's disappearance or not. She saw no sign that the teenagers had been here. But Lorenzo had a feeling, and Eoin trusted that Lorenzo's feelings were based on observation, not premonition.

She turned to Lorenzo. "We need to figure out what you saw. It's beginning to feel like all clues point to the Cape May Marina."

38

"You must be joking." Dennis greeted them with his usual warmth.

"I know it sounds crazy," Anna explained again. "But two teenagers are missing. You must have seen the police cars going around town, and something is odd about one of your boats."

Dennis raised an eyebrow. "But you don't know which one."

Anna bit her lip. It was true. Lorenzo had noticed something odd about the dock, or possibly one of the boats on it, but he didn't know what. It just made his trouble sense tingle.

Dennis shook his head and let out a long breath. "Look, you're all bonkers as far as I'm concerned, but if it'll make you feel better, sure. Let's go have a look, shall we?"

He pulled his office door shut behind him, turning his back on them to lock it with a key from the ring dangling from his belt. Satisfied it was secure, he looked back at them. "So, how do we do this?"

"Come on," Eoin called, already running ahead of them along the pier.

At each berth, Eoin peered over the edge into the murky water then crouched to look along the length of the boat.

Impressed by his choices, Anna followed suit, carefully examining each berth in turn. Lorenzo and Dennis followed, Dennis scoffing periodically, Lorenzo nervously twisting his hands.

"I am so sorry I can't tell you more," Lorenzo said once again. "Something is off. I can feel it."

"No, you saw it," Eoin said patiently. "You saw something, and it's in the back of your mind." He looked up at the worried man and smiled. "You'll remember. You'll see."

"Try not to think about it," Anna added. "That usually works for me. If I stop forcing myself to think about something, I'm more likely to remember it."

Lorenzo nodded and looked out over the water. If the worry reflected in his eyes was any indication, he had failed to stop thinking about it.

They checked each boat in turn, but nothing stood out. Nobody hung from the pier into the water. Nobody was visibly tied up on a boat. Nobody called out for help.

At the end of the pier, they all stopped and looked back the way they had come. Anna put her hands on her hips and stared at the boats. Dennis laughed under his breath. Eoin pulled out his notebook and flipped through the pages.

"There!" Anna shouted, pointing.

"What? Where?" Lorenzo grabbed her arm.

"Brad's boat. I saw a flash of light."

"Nah." Dennis waved his hand. "The boat's just rocking in the waves. You must've seen sunlight reflecting off the windows."

"It's true. The curtains are closed tight," Lorenzo added as they approached the boat. "You couldn't have seen light from inside."

"There are some cracks in the curtains. It's possible. Plus, why are the curtains even closed?" Anna asked. "They were all tied back last time I was on board."

Dennis shrugged. "There's nobody on board. So they closed the curtains. What's odd about that?"

A faint sound cut through the air.

"BethAnne!" Eoin shouted.

"That was a yell. I heard it!" Anna grabbed Lorenzo by the arm. "Do you think they're on there?"

"Calm down!" Dennis shouted too. "That was just a kid shrieking at the pool across the way. We hear them all the time. It really annoys the toffs. They're demanding some kind of soundproof wall between them and us."

"That wasn't from the pool," Anna insisted. "That came from this boat. I'm sure of it." She walked along the side of the boat, calling out, "BethAnne, are you there?"

Eoin followed behind her then clambered up onto the deck. "It's locked. Look." He pointed at the sliding door leading into the main cabin. A padlock had been installed that prevented the door from sliding.

"Hello?" Anna banged on the glass. The glass remained dark, the blue curtain inside pulled fully across it, blocking anything from view. "If someone's in there, they're locked in. Dennis, we need your keys—or someone else's keys that can get us into this boat."

"My keys?" Dennis looked back and forth between Anna and Lorenzo. "Lady, I'm not giving you my keys."

Eoin tugged at Dennis's trousers and looked up at him with his eyes wide. "Please, sir, my best friend might be trapped in there."

His best friend! Anna couldn't help but smile at that.

She hoped BethAnne felt the same way, though she had her doubts. "We don't know for sure, but two children are missing. So it's possible... well, they might have somehow got themselves locked in there."

Dennis shook his head. "There's no way. I would see if someone was brought onto that boat against their will. Any boat. And it's more than my job is worth to go bursting into someone else's yacht."

"Then why is it locked like that?" Lorenzo pointed out. "Isn't that unusual?"

Dennis turned to face Lorenzo, his hands balled into fists and raised slightly. "Don't you think if your friends were in there, they'd be calling out and banging on the door? You think they're just sitting there, twiddling their thumbs?"

All Anna's muscles tightened. He was right. If they were in there, they should be making noise, trying to get out. But what if they weren't able to move? Or call out? What if they were unconscious?

Eoin spoke up again. "Please, sir, please." He grabbed Dennis's hands and practically dragged him onto the boat.

Anna stepped close to the boat, trying to hear any noise from inside. She heard nothing. Was this a wild goose chase? Why on earth had she thought Lorenzo's feeling and this boat were in any way connected?

With a loud sigh, Dennis pulled the key ring off his belt and flipped through the keys.

The first key didn't fit the lock. "Huh, that's weird. That's the master for all our locks." He continued working through the keys on his chain, rejecting each key that didn't fit, jiggling those that he could insert, trying to open the lock. Finally, he looked back at Anna and Eoin. None of the keys unlocked the padlock.

39

Lorenzo and Dennis huddled at the edge of the parking lot, talking quietly. Anna couldn't hear them but didn't really care. She continued pacing up and down at the entrance to the parking lot. She'd called Evan at least two minutes ago. Where was he?

"Where is he?" Eoin echoed her thoughts. He paced directly behind her, matching her steps, turning when she did.

She pulled him close and hugged him tightly. "He'll be here any second now. I promise."

A shriek carrying from the pool next door caught her attention. They really did make a lot of noise. What if the sound she'd heard earlier really was from the pool? What if she was getting worked up about nothing? Worse, what if they broke into Brad's boat, and no one was there, and Brad sued her?

She squeezed Eoin even tighter. She had no choice. She had to do something.

She jumped up and pulled Eoin to the side as Evan's

police car raced into the lot. He swung across a space and jumped out of the car.

"Show me!" he called as he jogged toward the marina.

Anna and Eoin ran after him, catching up as he paused in front of Brad's boat.

He jumped on board and examined the door and the lock. "Is this how this boat is typically locked?" he called to Dennis.

"No, sir," Dennis replied. "Those doors are fitted with dead bolts that can be locked from inside or outside with a key. No reason to use a padlock." He paused, scratching his chin. "Unless the dead bolt is broken. Maybe this is just a temporary fix."

Anna jumped up next to Evan, Eoin close behind her. "I think I heard someone calling out from inside, and I saw a flash of light."

"It was a call from the pool at the next marina," Dennis called up to them, "and sunlight reflecting on the window. Nothing more."

"We're trying to contact Brad." Evan glanced at his watch. "I haven't heard back from headquarters yet. I don't know if they've found him."

"Evan. Please." Anna put a hand on his arm.

Eoin looked up at the officer, his round eyes filled with tears.

Evan only took a second. With a firm nod, he jumped down and jogged to his car, returning immediately with bolt cutters. "Stand back and stay behind me." With a sharp crack, the heavy tool cut through the padlock. Evan jerked the door free and pulled it open, pushing his way through the closed curtains beyond.

"Stay here," Anna whispered to Eoin then followed Evan in.

Anna found the main cabin empty. The heavy curtains

kept the room dark, but Anna could see two glasses standing in the small sink, the remains of what looked like soda pooling in them. She heard Evan's soft steps coming from the stairs down to the cabins and tiptoed after him.

At the bottom of the steps, Evan stopped in front of another closed door. This one didn't seem locked. He glanced back at her and put a finger to his lips. He braced himself, widening his stance and putting one hand on his weapon, the other on the doorknob. Without another sound, he swung the door open, lunging inside. Then he stopped.

Anna jumped forward to peer around him. Two sets of teenage eyes looked up at Evan in terror.

❧ 40 ❧

BethAnne dragged the heavy black headphones she wore away from one ear. "What's going on?" Her eyes flicked to Anna. "Ms. McGregor, are you okay?"

"Am I okay?" Anna called, pushing Evan aside and forcing her way into the room. She sensed Evan leaving the cabin but focused her attention on the teenagers. "Beth-Anne! David! We've been so worried about you!"

"Worried?" David pulled his own headphones off.

Behind him, Anna saw flashes of red and yellow light as soldiers on the screen continued shooting at each other even after the teenagers turned away. She could hear the sound of shots, the shouts of the characters, the pulsating music that accompanied the game. No wonder the teens hadn't heard them calling. She was amazed they had any hearing left at all.

BethAnne dropped her control stick and stood up. "Of course we're okay. Unless you count my kicking David's butt in this game not okay. But that's normal, isn't it?" she teased him.

David grinned and nodded. "I thought I'd have better luck on this system."

"You've been in here playing video games?" Evan reentered the room, seeming to have satisfied himself there was no one else on the boat.

BethAnne shrugged. "Sure, why not? David's parents told him he could come over here. It's their neighbor's boat."

"David's parents have no idea where you are," Evan said. "And I don't think this is his neighbor's boat."

"So, what happened?" Anna asked Evan, standing with both arms wrapped protectively around the kids.

"Come on. We can sort this out later." Evan shepherded them all out of the cabin. "Let's get you both home."

Back out on the pier, Evan radioed in to announce his find as Eoin filled BethAnne and David in on the ongoing search for them.

BethAnne pulled her cell phone from her heavy backpack, and her eyes opened wide. "Twenty calls from my mom. I was so focused on the game I didn't even feel the phone vibrate. I can't believe it. I thought David's parents knew. They told us we could go." BethAnne looked up at Anna. "I'm so sorry to have caused all this trouble."

"It's okay, sweetheart. Don't worry about that now." Anna pulled Evan to one side. "At least now you know it wasn't Lorenzo. He wouldn't have called me if he was the one who'd locked them in there."

"Maybe not," Evan replied. "But I have to wonder, did Lorenzo find them, or did he put them there?"

"Oh, Evan. Anyone who knew what David heard could have done that. Someone found out that he'd heard something that night. The killer got nervous and panicked."

"It's Brad's boat, so he's clearly in the picture," Evan said. "But Dennis has keys to the boat as well. Plus, as a local, he's more likely to have heard about what David knew through the gossip channel. But Luke is local too. And so is Lorenzo."

"I'm still so surprised that BethAnne would just disappear like that without telling anyone. It's not like her."

"The text message David got seemed real. Whoever sent it must have used one of those apps."

"Apps? What apps?"

Evan shook his head. "There are far too many. It's easy now to mask the number you're texting or calling from, even make it look like the message is coming from a different number. David thought his parents were okay with it. They even suggested he go to the yacht to play video games. What teenager would turn down an offer like that?"

A shout from the parking lot drew their attention. Evan jogged up to join the other officers who'd just arrived, bringing Brad with them.

Brad jumped out of the car before it stopped moving. "What's going on? What have you done to my boat?" His face glowed bright red in the afternoon sun, and sweat prickled along his upper lip. "If you've damaged anything, I'll sue..." He pulled free of the hand Evan had placed on his arm and ran down the pier to his boat.

"Mr. Atherton," Evan called as he chased him. "You need to calm down."

He finally caught up to Brad, spun him around, and held him still. "There's been an incident, Mr. Atherton. Two missing teenagers were found on your boat."

"Missing? On my boat? Did those vandals break in? Did they steal anything?"

"No, Mr. Atherton. They were lured there and locked in."

Brad looked thoroughly confused, and Anna felt momentary commiseration for him—only a moment.

"Did you lock them in there?" She marched up to him. "Did you lure them to your boat, two innocent, young people?"

Brad's confusion passed as quickly as it came, and he glared at her angrily. "What is she doing here?" He looked back at Evan. "Officer, I insist you tell me what's going on. But she"—he pointed at Anna—"has no reason to be here."

Evan kept his eyes on Brad but nodded at Anna. "You better go back up to the cars. Wait for me there."

Anna shoved her hands in her pockets and nodded. She trudged back up the pier to the parking lot, where Beth-Anne's and David's parents were tearfully squeezing their children to death. Eoin jumped up and down, laughing, as David tried to explain to his parents that he was never actually missing and everything was fine.

Brad was right. Anyone could have sent that text message, locked the teenagers up on the boat, and been planning to do something horrible to them to keep David quiet. She trembled at the thought.

❧ 41 ❧

"Thanks, Evan." Anna paused by the open car door, watching as Eoin bounced up the steps of Climbing Rose Cottage.

They'd accepted the ride home from Evan, Eoin too excited to walk and Anna to exhausted after her early start and terrifying afternoon. The day had been one long roller coaster, and not the fun kind.

"Look, I need to get back to the station. Lots of paperwork to do now." Evan grinned. "But you saved them, you know? If you hadn't been so insistent, I wouldn't have broken in. And if we hadn't found them in time, who knows what the kidnapper had in store for them?" He leaned across the car and took Anna's hand. "Go inside. Take a bath or something. Just relax. And know that you were a hero today, okay?"

Anna nodded and waved as Evan drove away. She didn't feel like a hero. She trudged up the porch steps and into the house, making it as far as the lounge before she collapsed onto the sofa. At least her day was over. She'd left afternoon tea out for guests to help themselves, and a few dirty teacups waited for her on the sideboard, but other than that, she could do exactly what Evan suggested—take a long, hot bath and go to bed.

She closed her eyes for just a moment.

"Ahem. Anna? Anna?"

Her arm shook as someone nudged her. "What? Who?" Anna rubbed a hand over her eyes and looked around the dark room. "What happened? What's going on?"

Michael Chan stared down at her. Tara Blanch stood just behind him. The door to the kitchen swung open, and Eoin came in, munching on a cookie.

"What time is it?" she asked no one in particular.

"Seven. Why?" Michael replied with a question of his own. "I came by to see Tara. We were chatting, and she told me I should talk to you."

"Oh, right." Anna sat up and ran a hand through her hair, trying to straighten it out. Eoin rolled his eyes, making it clear she failed. "What can I do for you?"

"My dear, you look like you could use a cup of tea." Tara moved to the sideboard, where things were still set out for afternoon tea. "Let me make one for you."

While Tara rattled teacups and saucers, Michael sat down on the chair across from Anna. "I mentioned something about Luke to Tara, and she thought you should know."

"Luke?" Anna asked, her brow furrowing.

"I couldn't help but notice that the two of you are very close," Tara added.

Eoin climbed up on the sofa next to Anna, trailing chocolate chip cookie crumbs. Anna absentmindedly wiped the crumbs from the sofa into a pile then into her hand, depositing them on a coaster to throw away when she stood up.

"I saw him down at the boatyard," Michael said.

"Here you go, dear." Tara handed her a steaming cup, which Anna accepted gratefully.

"At the Cape May Marina?"

"No, the other one," Michael explained. "Bluff Point Boatyard. This morning, after we cleaned the boat from our fishing trip."

Eoin was watching them carefully and nodded. He nudged Anna.

"Sure, I remember," she said. "Luke was taking his boat to test it out."

"Right, well." Michael waved a hand to reject the cup of tea Tara handed him. "He was in a mood about something when he got there. That policeman—Evan? Tried to ask him some questions, and Luke practically lost it."

"What do you mean, lost it? He didn't hit Evan, did he?"

"Nah, I guess he's not that stupid, but he punched a wall. He put his hand clean through it, and I overheard one of the other cops saying that Luke was angrier than he admitted about the way Oliver treated him."

Tara took Michael's offered tea as her own and perched on a chair near the window. She sipped and watched, her eyes moving back and forth between Michael and Anna. Apparently, a keen sense of observation was something she and Eoin had in common.

"What? Why would Luke be so angry at Oliver?" Anna asked.

Michael grinned. "It seems this wasn't the first time Oliver had been rude to him. Anyway." He stood up. "I just wanted you to know that guy has a temper."

Anna tried to laugh. She stood, too, placing her empty cup on a side table. "I know Luke well enough. You don't need to worry."

She walked Michael out then came back to the lounge,

where Tara and Eoin were engaged in a discussion about appropriate historiographical methods. Eoin was definitely not a typical eight-year-old. Anna made a mental note to ask her parents what they knew about why Eoin had been sent to Cape May earlier than planned and why his parents were willing to part with him for so long.

She carried the dirty teacups into the kitchen and got to work, hand-washing the china cups and plates she'd used that afternoon. A soft bump on her leg followed by a loud meow alerted her to Tough Cookie's desire to be fed.

"Right, your turn." She picked up the cat and made her way to a cabinet to find the cat food. "I told Michael I wasn't worried." She dug through the cabinet for the can and bowl. "But I am worried. Aren't you?" She looked Tough Cookie in the eye as she placed the cat back on the floor. "All I've done since I got involved in this is make it worse."

She put the bowl of food in front of the cat then squatted to pet her while she ate. "Lorenzo is a really strong suspect. He has a motive. He has a track record of breaking the law. But he's a good neighbor. Why would he attack BethAnne? That doesn't make any sense."

Tears welled in her eyes, so she tried to focus on the cat. "You know what's going on. Don't you? Cats know these things. I wish you could tell me."

The kitchen door swung open, and from the corner of her eye, she saw Eoin approach. Embarrassed about her tears, she didn't turn to face him. "Good talk with Ms. Blanch?"

Eoin crouched next to her and put his arm around her waist. "It's okay, Cousin Anna. I'll help you. We'll figure it out."

Anna couldn't help but laugh at the comfort she drew

from Eoin's hug, from Tough Cookie's purr. All she'd accomplished was putting people she cared about in danger. She was so sure she could protect herself that she hadn't stopped to think about protecting others. She hugged Eoin tight and let her tears flow.

❧ 42 ❧

Anna's guests enjoyed breakfast on the porch again the next morning. Clear skies let the sun cast a bright glow along the roses as their scent wafted up to the tables. Birds chirped from the ancient trees that lined the property as a slight breeze ruffled their leaves. Anna tried to let the beauty of the morning bring her the joy it usually did, but the sight of Tara Blanch sitting alone, picking at her breakfast scone, reminded Anna of the danger that still lurked in town.

"Got everything you need?" Anna forced her voice into a happy chirp as she addressed Tara. "Can I bring you anything? Another cup of coffee?"

"Yes, thank you. That would be lovely." Tara nodded without looking at Anna.

Anna bit her lip as she went back through to the kitchen to get the fresh pot. When she returned to the porch, Eoin had joined Tara at her table.

"Eoin, don't bother Ms. Blanch. I'm sure she'd rather be alone."

"Oh no, it's no bother." Tara beamed at Eoin. "I enjoy talking to this young man. Quite precocious, isn't he?"

"Indeed," Anna replied, eyeing Eoin warily.

He offered her his most innocent smile as he reached into his pants pocket and pulled out his notebook.

Anna placed the coffee pot on the sideboard, said goodbye to the other guests as they returned to their rooms, then came back to Tara and Eoin.

"Tara." She leaned down on an empty chair. "I'd love to learn more about your writing. I'm afraid I haven't read much of it. I suppose I should have."

"Please." Tara waved away the suggestion. "You read what you want to read. There's no reason to feel you have to read one thing or to feel guilty about reading another."

"I started one of your stories last night," Eoin piped up, his smile so big all of his teeth showed.

"You did? Well! I should warn you I don't write children's stories."

Anna laughed as she moved away to clear the other tables. "Don't worry about Eoin. Like you said, he's way ahead of his age." She returned, holding a stack of plates. "But why do you spend time with Oliver Humphreys-Gibbons—I mean—why did you?"

Tara's smile vanished. Her eyes narrowed. "Yes. Did. Exactly. Such a tragedy. He was a good man, a good friend."

"Ladies. Eoin." Luke greeted them as he came around from the side of the house.

The sight of Luke brought an image to Anna's mind of how angry he'd gotten the last time she'd seen him. Jealous, Eoin had said. Furious had been Michael's choice of words. With a start at the memory, Anna's grip on the plates loosened. Just for a second, but it was enough. The stack of plates cascaded forward, sliding one over the other until they crashed to the floor.

Luke jumped forward and reached for the plates, but he was too late. "Let me help." He got down on one knee and picked through the remains of the plates. "They're not all broken."

"I can't believe I did that," Anna groaned as she joined Luke on her knees. She reached for the plates that were still whole, placing them carefully on the sideboard.

Luke gathered the larger pieces then stood. "We'll just sweep up the last of these. Come on. I'll help you carry those." He grabbed the stack Anna had put on the sideboard and headed inside.

"I'm so sorry about that," Anna mumbled as she followed Luke into the kitchen.

"What was that about?" Luke slotted the plates into the dishwasher. "You looked like you'd seen a ghost." He dropped the last plate into place and came over to Anna. "Is it that woman? What's her name, Donna White? Are you scared of her?"

Anna took a step back from Luke then tried to lean casually against the table as if she hadn't been backing away from him. "No, not at all. Though I do want to know more about her."

"Her? Why?"

Anna took a breath then dropped onto a chair. "You know what happened to BethAnne and David, right?"

Luke joined her at the table. "Yeah, I heard about that. Creepy. But they're both fine, right? They were just playing video games."

"They're okay, but who would have lured them away like that? And why?"

Luke raised one shoulder but averted his eyes.

Anna could understand. It wasn't a nice thought. "What if it was the killer—the person who killed Oliver—and he just wanted to keep the kids hidden, then he was going to come back at night and kill them too?"

Luke reached across the table and took her hand. "It's okay, Anna. They're okay. You're safe. I'm here, and I'll make sure you stay safe."

Anna held her breath. "You will?"

"Of course. Why do you even have to ask?"

Anna sighed. "Luke, I've heard stories. About you getting really angry at Evan. I just wondered..."

Luke look confused. "Wondered what?"

"Oh, never mind." Anna put her other hand into Luke's. "Look, you must understand it's more important than ever to find out what's going on, now that BethAnne and David are in danger. BethAnne's parents took her out of town for a few days, to get away and relax, so that's something at least. But still..."

"I see." Luke dropped her hands and leaned back in his chair, hooking his thumbs in the front pockets of his jeans. "But why do you need to be involved? David's talked to the police. And thanks to what happened, they must be taking his evidence seriously."

Anna nodded. "I know. It's true. But last night, I thought maybe I'd only made things worse by sticking my nose in. I've talked to a lot of people about the murder."

"Like who?"

"Brad Atherton, Michael, Tara—I mean Donna White, Steve. You saw him." Anna ticked off the names as she said them. "At least I've had some fun with it. Michael took me and Sammy fishing, and I got to hang out on Brad's yacht and try a Bee's Knees."

"Bee's Knees?" Luke raised an eyebrow. "I've heard of those. A classic cocktail, right?"

Anna nodded, looking down. "I shouldn't be having fun. This is serious."

Luke leaned forward again. "It is serious. But don't get down about it. I don't like you getting involved—don't get me wrong—but I'm sure that if you are doing something, it's helpful. It's not hurting people."

Anna smiled. "I guess, in one way, Evan was right. If I hadn't stuck my nose in, we might not have found them."

"Evan is right, huh?" Luke pushed up from the table. "Of course he is. I'm sure Evan is always right."

Anna held her breath. Was this going to be some kind of outburst?

But when Luke turned back to her, he grinned. "Don't worry, Anna. I'm not scared off by a little competition. You do what you need to do. And know that I'll be here if you need me." He leaned down and pecked her on the cheek. "That's what friends are for, right?"

Anna raised one hand to her cheek as she watched him leave. How could she have been so wrong about him? She'd let the gossip get to her. She still had so much to learn about the people in this town. Starting with Tara Blanch. But by the time she went back out to the porch with the broom and dustpan, Tara and Eoin were gone.

43

Sunlight filtered through the leaves painting shadows that danced on the sidewalks. Neighbors smiled and waved, calling friendly greetings as she passed. She took a few breaths and forced herself to smile.

Eoin's note had been simple, neat. It didn't look like he'd been under any kind of stress when he wrote it. And why wouldn't the two history lovers go see the Physick House together? It was a famous historical landmark, home of Dr. Emlen Physick, exactly the sort of place Eoin would love, and probably somewhere Tara Blanch had visited often.

But given what had happened just yesterday, Anna couldn't keep her anger toward Tara from rising. What was she thinking, taking an eight-year-old boy off without getting Anna's permission first? Who did that woman think she was?

She took another calming breath as she returned a friendly wave from another neighbor but picked up her pace. She needed to see Eoin and make sure he was safe.

Movement to her right drew her attention to the tennis

courts near the historic house. She slowed her pace enough to identify the four people playing at the court nearest the street. They laughed and joked, taking the game seriously but not too seriously, just the way Anna would if she were playing. One of them noticed her, waved, and trotted over.

"Want to join the game?" he asked.

"Minister Woodley." Anna smiled. "It looks like you're having a great time. It's a perfect day for it."

"It's a glorious day." Minister Woodley smiled, then his face sobered. "I was so sorry to hear about the incident with the teenagers yesterday. Terrible news. Thank the Lord they're both safe. Who could have done such a mean thing? Locking them on a boat like that?"

Anna wondered exactly what the local gossip mill was saying about the event. As far as Anna was concerned, it was a kidnapping. But BethAnne and David had gone to the boat of their own free will. They hadn't even realized they were locked in. What kind of charges would the police be able to bring against whoever had done it?

"I have to admit, I'm surprised to see him here, ready to play tennis as if nothing had happened." Minister Woodley pointed his racket toward two men waiting on the far side of the court. "They have the court booked after us." A call from one of the minister's fellow players distracted him. "Duty calls. I must get back to the game. We only have the court for about five more minutes." He waved again and trotted back to his team.

Anna's brow furrowed, and her jaw jutted out. She needed to check that Eoin was safe with Tara, but she also needed to know what Brad had to say about how her friends had ended up on his boat—and what he was going to do about it. She pushed her sleeves up and marched around to their side of the court. "Brad. Michael."

"Not you again." Brad let out a loud sigh.

Michael just nodded.

"Having a pleasant morning?" Anna asked with a smile.

"Not exactly, no thanks to you," Brad snapped back.

"We've been kicked off the boat," Michael explained. "We can't go back on until the police are done searching it."

"I have no idea why they need to search my boat." Brad sniffed and picked at his racket strings. "There's nothing there to help them. *I* don't know who convinced those kids to break into my boat. I should be getting compensation for the mess they made, not being made to suffer like this."

Suffer? Anna's anger rose, and she took another breath. "It doesn't look like you're suffering too badly." She let her sarcasm ring loud and clear. "Aren't you curious about why somebody lured them to *your* boat?"

Brad raised an eyebrow at her then looked away without answering.

Michael shrugged and smiled. "It was just a coincidence, of course. It must have been. They had to choose somewhere with a gaming system, and Brad's boat was convenient."

"How would anyone even know Brad had a gaming system down in his office?" Anna asked.

Michael shrugged again and glanced at Brad. "A lot of people have been on that boat in the past few days. Guests, cleaning staff, marina staff."

"And the people who came over for the party the night Oliver died," Anna added.

Brad inhaled sharply, but he still didn't respond. Apparently he was taking his decision to not talk to her seriously.

Michael laughed. "Yeah, them too. But I don't see any of them being involved in a trick like that."

"Or a murder?" Anna asked.

"Murder? You think the two things are connected?"

Anna nodded. "Absolutely. David heard something the

night Oliver was killed. He might have given the police the evidence they need to figure out who did it."

"Well, like I said, none of the guests from that night were involved. I don't think any of them even went below. Did they, Brad?"

Brad just wrinkled one lip.

"Right," Michael continued. "We got to the boat a little late, since I had to stop and pick up the gin." He shot a sideways look at Anna and winked. "You remember the gin, Brad?"

Brad's face turned an odd shade of puce, but Michael didn't seem to care. "Ha. I just made it to the liquor store before it closed at nine. And by the time we got to the boat, Brad had everything already set out."

"Someone might have gone down to use the head, Michael," Brad said through gritted teeth.

"Right. Obviously."

"But I have no idea why you're sitting here gossiping like this. Come on. Our court is free," Brad added.

Michael winked at Anna again, grabbed his racket, and trotted out onto the court after Brad.

Anna watched them go, wondering. Why was Brad so reluctant to talk to her? Wasn't that suspicious in itself?

"Don't be silly," she said to herself. "No one has to talk to you, you know. You're not actually a detective."

"Maybe not," she answered herself. "But I'm going to find out where Eoin is and if he's safe." Anna jogged the last few yards to the Physick House.

44

"I'm sorry. I don't want to buy a ticket. I'm not really visiting the house." Anna balled her hands into fists as she tried to explain the situation to the gray-haired woman waving a ticket in her face. "I'm looking for my young cousin."

"If you don't want to visit, then why are you trying to get in?"

Anna let out a breath in exasperation. "Can you just tell me if there's a little redheaded boy in here, Irish accent, talks a lot?"

"Oh, him." The old woman's face creased into a smile. "What a darling boy. Yes, he's inside."

"Thank goodness." Anna slumped back against the door. "I just need to see him, make sure he's okay. He ran off without talking to me."

"A runaway?" The woman's face fell. "But he's so happy. He loves the house. And he's with a woman—I thought she was his mother."

Anna rolled her eyes. "Not his mother. Not even a

friend. She's just a guest at my B and B. I run Climbing Rose Cottage."

"Louise's niece?" The woman's smile reappeared. "Of course you are. I'm sorry I didn't recognize you, dear. Please, do come in and find the young boy. I believe I saw them heading upstairs."

Anna thanked her profusely and ducked inside, heading straight for the stairs. Halfway up, she could already hear Eoin's chatter.

"...And it became soda, and he was Dr. Emlen's grandfather, and he was a doctor, so people trusted him, and he was rich, and look at that table. It's typical for this style..."

Anna burst into the bedroom where Eoin and Tara leaned over a display table.

"Eoin!" Anna called, grabbing him and hugging him.

"Cousin Anna?" Eoin wriggled free and stepped back. "Are you okay?"

"I'm fine, honey." Anna glared at Tara. "You need to ask me before you go running off like that."

Eoin's brow furrowed. He stepped forward and took Anna's hand. "But I left a note."

"Yes, you did. Thank you for that. But it's not enough. You're too young to go off with a stranger."

"A stranger!" Tara's eyes widened. "I'm hardly a stranger."

Anna took another calming breath. She was going to hyperventilate at this rate. "I understand that I know who you are, but I don't really know you. And I don't appreciate you taking Eoin away from the house without asking my permission."

"I see." Tara folded her hands in front of herself. "Then I suggest you take him home."

Anna nodded and pulled Eoin back down the stairs and out of the house.

He trotted along next to her willingly but with questions. "What happened? I don't understand. Don't you want me to see this house? It's an amazing place. I can learn so much about Cape May here, about history, about medicine."

Anna waited until they were out in the parking lot before kneeling down and hugging Eoin one more time. "I know, honey, and we'll come back here again. I promise. It's a great place to visit. But you must understand that I was really worried about you, especially after what happened yesterday."

Eoin's eyes fell. "I'm sorry, Cousin Anna."

"Good boy." Anna gave him one more hug before standing. "Come on. Let's get home."

Before they could leave the parking lot, Eoin pulled her arm in the opposite direction. "Look, it's Patrolman Evan."

Anna looked to where Eoin eagerly pointed. Evan stood in the small tent that served as a coffee shop just outside the house. Anna let Eoin drag her over.

"Hey there." Evan came over to pat Eoin on the head and give Anna a quick peck on the cheek. "My two favorite people. What brings you here?"

"Oh... nothing..." Anna's eyes moved around the small eating area as she tried to decide how much to tell Evan about what Tara had done. "Eoin really wanted to see this house, so he ran over here without me." She looked down at Eoin, who blushed.

"I said I was sorry."

Evan frowned but patted Eoin's head again. "As long as he's okay. Listen, Anna, I wanted to talk to you."

"About what?"

Evan glanced around then bent down and handed Eoin a five-dollar bill. "Eoin, why don't you go over there and get yourself one of those big donuts?"

Eoin's eyes lit up. He grabbed the proffered bill and trotted over to the counter.

Anna kept her eyes on Eoin as she followed Evan to a nearby table.

"We learned something about your friend Steve."

Anna tore her eyes away from Eoin as she laughed. "He's hardly my friend." Then she narrowed her eyes. "What did you learn?"

"Detective Walsh got it out of him during an interview. He's got a past relationship with the victim."

"With Oliver? But I already knew they were friends."

"Friends?" Evan raised an eyebrow. "If that's what he told you, he wasn't being entirely truthful. Quite the opposite, in fact. Steve applied for a joint appointment with the linguistics department. Oliver blocked his appointment."

"Oh. But then why did he talk about him like they were friends? Michael said Steve followed Brad and Oliver around. Steve even bragged about their friendship."

Evan shook his head. "That's something we need to figure out. I just wanted to tell you. In case you had any ideas about..."

"About what?" Anna leaned forward.

"Well..." Evan toyed with the lace tablecloth. "About getting back together with him or something like that."

Eoin appeared at Anna's side, his face and hands covered in sticky white icing.

"Oh, Eoin, you're a mess." Anna pulled a paper napkin from the holder on the table and tried without success to wipe him clean. She glanced at Evan. "Don't worry about that. There's no chance. Believe me. And I'm not shocked that I didn't know something else about Steve. It seems like I find out new things about him every day."

Evan stood then took a step back from the sticky boy in front of him. "I'm glad to hear that. We're going to keep digging into all the suspects, of course. But I do feel like we're getting closer. Every little bit of information helps." He leaned down to give Anna another peck on the cheek, waved to Eoin—keeping his distance from the boy's gooey hands—and headed out.

"What did Patrolman Evan want?" Eoin asked as he licked each of his fingers in turn.

"Just to let me know that they're moving forward with their investigation into how Oliver died. It seems they have more suspects now."

"That's good." Eoin pulled at the bits of paper napkin that had stuck to his fingers and dropped the bits into his pocket. "Cousin Anna, I'm really sorry I upset you. I didn't mean to."

"I know, honey. Come on. Let's get you home and washed up."

She was glad to know Lorenzo wasn't their only suspect anymore, but she didn't like that the new information meant she would have to have another difficult conversation with Steve.

❃ 45 ❃

"Hello, anybody home?" Sammy's voice rang out through Climbing Rose Cottage.

"Sammy!" Eoin ran to greet her at the door, drying his freshly washed hands on his shirt as he ran. He grabbed her hand in his and dragged her back to the kitchen.

"This is a surprise. Why aren't you at the bakery?" Anna asked.

"Paperwork." Sammy rolled her eyes. "My accountant had issues with renewing my business license, and now I need to go to the county offices in person to sort things out. So"—she held up a picnic basket—"I figured I might as well start with lunch with my two favorite people. I brought sandwiches."

Eoin jumped up to peer into the basket. "Oooh. Where shall we go for our picnic?"

Anna laughed. "It's turning into a picnicky type of week. We stayed home last time, so let's go somewhere fun this time. How about a park?"

"Perfect." Sammy nodded. "I noticed on the drive over that Harbor View Park has benches and tables."

"I just need to make one call first," Anna said.

"Cousin Anna." Eoin let a whine creep into his voice. "Let's go eat."

"Okay, okay, this won't take long. I promise."

She ran into the lounge and grabbed her phone. She paused for a second when she realized she still had Steve's number in her phone's favorites list. That needed to change, but first, she needed to call him.

Her call went right to voicemail. "Steve, it's Anna. I need to talk to you. I have some things... well, just some things I need to know. Can you call me? Or if you want, I'll be having lunch over at Harbor View Park. You can find me there."

"Really? You want him to join us for lunch?"

Anna spun around to see Sammy leaning against the door from the kitchen, her arms folded across her chest. Eoin stuck his head around the corner then came through the door and stood next to Sammy, mimicking her pose.

"Stop it, both of you." Anna wagged her finger. "I don't *want* to talk to Steve. I have to, for the investigation."

"Uh-huh. That better be true, honey. Or else..." Sammy wagged her finger right back at Anna.

Laughing, Anna grabbed a sun hat. "Come on. Let's go."

The trio set off in Sammy's car, parking just outside the small park that looked out over the bay and its various marinas. Other people had had the same idea—not surprising given the gorgeous day—but they managed to find a bench for themselves. Anna and Sammy settled down to eat while Eoin grabbed his sandwich then skipped over to the wooden fence that lined the edge of the green. He peered down into the water, occasionally dropping bits of bread into the marina.

"Thanks for this. I'm sorry you have such a miserable afternoon planned, but I'm glad you decided to start it this way." Anna spoke with her mouth full of cured ham and cheese then wiped a drop of mustard off her lip.

"I'll always be here for you. You know that." Sammy leaned over to pat Anna on the leg. "I heard what happened to those kids. It's terrible."

Anna nodded. "Thank God they're okay, but I hate to think…"

"Then don't think about it. They're both fine now, and the police will figure out who did that to them."

Anna shrugged. "Maybe. But that's why I need to talk to Steve. Oh, how's that for timing?"

She dropped her sandwich into her napkin and wiped off her fingers as she stood to watch the couple coming toward them.

"Anna," Steve spoke first. "I got your message."

Anna nodded but pinched her lips together in frustration. "I see that. And you brought Coral along."

"We were together when you called, dear," Coral said in a sickly-sweet voice.

"Right… uh… just hanging out…" Steve's voice dropped off.

"Steve said he was going to come out and meet you here, and I saw no reason I shouldn't come along and enjoy the beautiful day as well." Coral smiled, revealing creases in her peach lipstick.

"Right, of course," Steve mumbled, running a hand through his hair. "The thing is, Anna, I was hoping we could talk. I was so glad when you called."

Coral's eyes opened wide. "You don't mean without me, do you?"

"Well… uh… um…"

Anna couldn't help smiling at Steve's discomfort, but

eventually she put him out of his misery. "I don't need to talk to you alone, Steve. Frankly, I don't want to be alone with you."

"Oh." He looked over as if seeing Sammy and Eoin for the first time.

They glared back.

"Sammy, this is my former advisor, Steve—"

"Don't bother." Sammy waved a hand. "I know who he is."

"Oh. Right. And of course you met Eoin when you came to the house."

"Hello, Eoin." Steve nodded down at the boy.

"Eoin," Eoin corrected Steve in a soft, sad voice that made it clear he had no expectations Steve would get it right.

Anna took a breath. "Steve, I wanted to talk to you because I need to ask you about Oliver."

Coral stepped closer to Steve and wrapped one arm through his. "Ooh, we're chatting about the murder? You are getting quite close to that dashing police officer. Aren't you?"

Steve's jaw moved as he gritted his teeth, and red splotches appeared on his cheeks.

Anna smiled. "Yes, as a matter of fact, I am. But this doesn't have to do with him. Look, Steve, I heard... through the grapevine... that you weren't as close to Oliver as you said."

"I don't know what you're talking about. I even considered a joint appointment with the linguistics department at one point."

"Right, but Oliver didn't approve it, did he? In fact, I heard he was the one who blocked you."

"Did you hear this from the police?" Steve's eyes narrowed, and he took a step toward Anna. "That's unprofessional behavior. They can't share information I give them privately."

"First of all," Sammy jumped in, "nothing you say to the police has to remain private. It might prove valuable information to use in court."

"Maybe so," Steve conceded. "But they still shouldn't gossip about it."

"Patrolman Evan would never gossip," Eoin said.

"No, of course he wouldn't," Anna replied, uncomfortable with the way the conversation was going, knowing Steve was right, and feeling guilty that Evan had felt the need to tell her those details.

"Pillow talk, was it, dear?" Coral grinned wickedly.

Sammy barked out a laugh, and Eoin looked up at her, clearly confused.

"No, it most certainly was not." Anna put both hands on her hips. "Look, I just wanted to give you a chance to explain, Steve. To me, I mean."

"I don't see why he owes you any kind of explanation," Coral complained.

"I can speak for myself." Steve's voice rose as he turned to look down at Coral.

"If that's the way you're going to be about it, fine, explain away," Coral sniffed.

"Well... actually, you're right. I don't owe you any explanation, Anna," Steve said. "But since you ask, it's true. Oliver had some concerns about the appointment. But they were purely logistical, I assure you. Nothing personal against me or my research. Of course, after the whole hullabaloo last year, when... well, when you left..."

Anna's eyes grew wide. "Wait, you're blaming me for him rejecting you?"

"He did *not* reject me. The appointment is still under consideration."

Sammy put a finger on her lip. "If it's still under consideration, and Oliver is gone, then that means you have a better chance of getting what you want. Doesn't it?"

Steve frowned. "I would never think of it that way. Oliver was a great researcher."

Coral tugged on Steve's arm. "I think we should leave now. Don't you?"

❧ 46 ❧

"That was not fun." Anna packed up the last of their napkins and plates.

"I can't believe you were in love with him." Sammy shook her head as she took a balled-up napkin from Eoin.

"I'm just glad you were here." Anna smiled at her. "Both of you." She gave Eoin a quick hug.

"Like I said, honey, I'll always be here for you." She glanced at her watch. "Except right now. I better go over to those offices and get this over with. I'll see you both back at Climbing Rose Cottage later, okay?"

Eoin gave her a big hug then took Anna's hand as they watched Sammy walk back to her car.

"How about a walk?" Anna looked down at Eoin. "We still have time before afternoon tea."

Eoin nodded eagerly, so hand in hand, they walked along the harbor, waving at neighbors, tossing rocks into the water, trying to identify the different gulls that circled overhead. The snap of sails and jingle of masts reminded Anna of the various ideas she had for finishing up the

Harbor Room in Climbing Rose Cottage. The other items she'd purchased had been delivered. She just needed to arrange everything. A gust of wind pushed past them, and Anna put a hand up to stop her sun hat from blowing away.

Eoin tugged on her other arm. "Is BethAnne okay, d'you think?" He looked up at Anna.

"I know you're worried about her, Eoin. So am I. But yes, she's perfectly safe. She's with her parents, and I'm sure they're taking great care of her."

"That's good." He kicked at the gravel under their feet, his face downcast.

"If I know BethAnne, she probably can't wait to come home and get back into her research."

"Oh no." Eoin shook his head. "I'm sure that's not true."

"No? I would've thought... oh, well." Anna shrugged. "Maybe you're right. You know her better than I do."

"No." Eoin laughed. "I mean she won't wait to come back to get into her research because she'll still be doing it. Just because she's out of town doesn't mean she's not reading and studying."

Anna laughed. "Of course, you're right. What was I thinking?"

Looking around, she realized they had made it all the way to Bluff Point Boatyard and Cape May Marina. Shouts and yells carried from the pool to their left while large yachts rocked gracefully in the marina to their right.

"Look, there's Lorenzo." Eoin pointed toward the rows of piers behind the pool.

Lorenzo stood on the deck of a small boat at the near end of the first pier of Bluff Point Boatyard. "It looks like a fishing boat," Anna said, reminded of the vessel she'd been out on the previous morning.

Eoin pulled out his notebook and started writing, occasionally scratching his ear.

Anna watched him with a smile then looked back at Lorenzo. "I didn't realize Lorenzo was a fisherman."

"I love the idea of going fishing." Eoin looked up at her. "Will you take me next time? Maybe we could go with Lorenzo."

"I don't know. His boat doesn't look like it's designed to hold a lot of people."

"We'd fit. I'm small. I could catch a few fish." Tucking his notebook under his arm, Eoin mimed casting a fishing rod then fighting with his catch as he reeled it back in.

Anna laughed and applauded, then looked over to see Lorenzo tying a series of knots in a rope that lay along the length of the boat. The vessel had been fitted with a row of holders for fishing rods. A small, half-covered wheelhouse held the captain's seat but not much else. Buckets lined the inside edges of the boat, but she couldn't see any other seats or benches.

"I wonder what that rope is for," she said under her breath as her eyes fixated on the sight of Lorenzo's strong hands pulling the thick, rough rope tight, knot after knot. "He's a strong man. Isn't he?"

"Oh yes." Eoin nodded. "He told me that once, at a traveling show, he had to stop a runaway trailer. He was the only person who could stand in front of it and hold it while the other people put the blocks under the tires."

"Interesting. I know the police aren't focusing only on Lorenzo anymore when it comes to this murder, and that's good. But I don't know who they are focusing on, if anyone." She shook her head. "Too many people have motive and opportunity."

In response, Eoin flipped through the pages of his notebook.

Anna continued with her thought. "Lorenzo... Steve... Michael or Brad... even Luke. And I really think Tara is hiding something. Her presence in town right now is just too coincidental."

"She doesn't have a boat, and she's not strong enough to kill someone." Eoin's high voice cut into her train of thought.

"Eoin, how do you know that?"

"She told me she didn't have a boat."

"No, I mean about killing someone."

Eoin shrugged. "I heard what Patrolman Evan said to you, Cousin Anna. It's also common sense."

"Ah. Clearly, I need to do a better job of protecting you from conversations like that."

Eoin shrugged then looked up at Anna with a sly grin. "I hear lots, y'know. My brother and sister are ages older than me."

"They are? I didn't remember that."

He nodded, his hair ruffling in the breeze. "They used to talk around me about all kinds of things."

"Used to?"

Eoin looked at the ground and kicked at a piece of gravel. "They moved out, y'know. It's just me, Ma, and Da now. And they don't talk to me much. They're too busy fighting with each other."

"Right. I see." And she did. She knelt down and wrapped Eoin in a bear hug. "I love having you here, Eoin. And I love talking to you—even if you sometimes hear things you probably shouldn't." She looked up then squinted in the direction of the Cape May Marina. "But since you're so smart, tell me this. If Tara doesn't have a boat, what's she doing talking to Dennis at the marina?"

❧ 47 ☙

"Come on." Anna took Eoin's hand and headed toward the Cape May Marina clubhouse.

Tara and Dennis stood close together, talking quietly, just outside the side entrance to the club. Tara had pushed her sunglasses to the top of her head and looked at Dennis intently, as if absorbing every word he said.

"Even if she doesn't have her own boat, she could have used someone else's. Or"—she put up a finger as Eoin opened his mouth to point out the problem with that theory—"she was working with someone else, maybe manipulating someone."

As she spoke, an image of Steve floated into her mind. She blinked and shook her head.

"Tara isn't a killer, Cousin Anna," Eoin replied quietly. "She's not."

Anna smiled down at him. "I know you like her, honey. I just need to know why she's sharing secrets with Dennis."

Anna didn't try to hide her presence, walking right up to the chatting couple. "Tara, I'm surprised to see you here. I didn't know you knew Dennis."

Tara sniffed and looked down her nose at Anna, then smiled as she turned her attention to Eoin. "Hello, Eoin dear. How are you? I'm sorry we didn't get to see the whole Physick House. We'll have to go back sometime." Her glare returned as she moved her attention back to Anna. "Not that it's any of your business, but I'm here looking for Brad."

"He's not here though, is he?" Dennis laughed lightly. "Locked off his own boat, ain't he?"

"I don't know why he's not allowed back on his boat," Tara objected. "As I was just saying before we were interrupted"—she glared at Anna again—"I see no indication of police activity on the boat."

"Just left, didn't they? They're probably calling him now to tell him to come back. You can wait for him if you want." Dennis waved toward the lounge, and Anna was surprised by his generosity.

"No, thank you." She slid her sunglasses back onto her nose then turned to Anna. "Did you want something else?"

"I thought you should know I didn't tell the police what you did with Eoin."

Tara's brow lowered, and she shook her head in bewilderment. "Tell the police? What I did?"

Dennis grinned but didn't interrupt, clearly enjoying the show.

"You took off with a young boy without my permission," Anna said.

"My dear, I took him to the Physick House. That's hardly the act of a hardened criminal."

"Right. And whoever lured those kids onto Brad's boat just had them playing video games, no harm done. Is that it?"

As if Anna's position had finally gotten through to her,

Tara's face blanched, and she put a hand over her mouth. "But... I didn't..."

Dennis, on the other hand, was getting angry himself. His eyes narrowed, and his face pinched closed. "What are you suggesting? That my marina isn't safe?"

"Just that it was used to kidnap two teenagers. Doesn't that bother you?"

"They weren't kidnapped. They were playing video games. They shouldn't have been there in the first place." Dennis looked away dismissively. "It's not my problem if they accidentally got locked in."

"Accidentally? Someone padlocked them in!" She let out a breath in frustration then tried a different approach. "Who could have locked the boat like that? Did you see Brad around the boat that afternoon?"

"Nah, I didn't see him." Dennis looked down as he answered then looked away across the marina, shuffling his feet.

Even Tara looked at him suspiciously. "What aren't you saying?"

"Look, I might have stepped away for a minute. No more. I had to meet someone."

Tara raised an eyebrow. "Who?"

"None of your business. Or yours." He poked a finger at Anna.

"My dear." Tara turned back to Anna. "I seem to owe you an apology. I wasn't thinking clearly. I do enjoy children so much. He was so excited to see the house, and you were busy cleaning up your mess..." She waved her hands gracefully, as if to paint a picture of the scene.

Anna recognized this as a rare moment of humanity from Tara, but she kept pushing. "Did you see Oliver the night he was killed?"

"Well, that's direct. No, I did not. I was with Brad all night. At dinner, then on his boat. We didn't see Oliver."

"Did you expect him?"

"Of course. I wouldn't have accepted Brad's invitation if I didn't expect Oliver to be there. But now, without Oliver..."

"Now you need Brad's help?"

Tara scoffed. "I don't need anyone's help. I do appreciate the feedback, getting updates on current research, but I can do that just as well by reading and attending conferences. No." She raised a hand to adjust her sunglasses. "I liked Oliver. He was my friend. I'm very sorry he's gone."

"So why are you looking for Brad?"

"I don't know." Tara frowned and shrugged. "Just to reach out. To be friendly."

"You?" Anna couldn't hide her surprise. "And you think Brad wants that?"

"No, I suppose you're right. Perhaps you know him better than I do." With that, Tara took a few steps toward the parking lot. Before she left, she turned back to Anna. "I hope you believe me. I never would have done anything to hurt Eoin. I am very sorry."

Dennis laughed out loud as they watched Tara make her way back to the parking lot. "Likes children, does she? Right. She doesn't like anyone, that one. She's as cold as ice."

❧ 48 ❧

More confused than ever, Anna followed Eoin as he skipped back to the parking lot between the two marinas. Lorenzo and his boat were nowhere to be seen, but Anna recognized another handsome boat—and a handsome man.

"Luke!" she called as she approached the dock. "How's the boat?"

Eoin ran along the pier and clambered up onto the boat uninvited. Luke didn't seem to mind. He just laughed as he gave Eoin a helping hand. "How you doing, buddy? Want to go out for a ride?"

"Yes! Yes!" Eoin jumped up and down, clapping his hands.

"Whoa." Luke put a hand on his shoulder to calm him down. "You can't act like that on a boat. You need to be careful. You could tip right over the edge."

Luke held out a strong arm to Anna. She grabbed it and let him half guide, half lift her onto the boat.

"It looks beautiful. It really does." She looked at the

polished wood glowing in the sunlight. "I'm so impressed by your work."

Luke stepped close behind her, his breath tickling her neck as he spoke. "I'm glad you're impressed. Ready to take her out with me?"

Anna shut her eyes and wrapped her arms around her body. "Sure, why not? I need a distraction right now, something to take my mind off this case so I can figure it out."

Luke stepped away from her, and she opened her eyes to see him casting the boat off from the dock. She slid onto one of the benches that lined the side of the boat and leaned forward over the edge into the wind as Luke guided the boat out of the marina and into the creek. She saw that the area where Oliver had been found was no longer marked off by police tape, though the large spot of trampled grasses and flattened mud still stood out from the rest of the space.

From the creek, they followed the canal out to the open ocean. Anna put a hand on her hat as the wind picked up and inhaled deeply the scents of salt and seaweed, fish and birds. Sprays of water caught her in the face, and she laughed, fully relaxed for the first time. For the first time since she'd put BethAnne in danger. She opened her eyes, and her face fell.

"What's on your mind?" Luke sidled up next to her. "It doesn't look good."

Anna shook her head. "I was just thinking about Beth-Anne and David. I need to help them. I need to figure this out."

"You need to take a break from the case. You said so yourself. Come on." He took her hand and led her to the back of the boat, where Eoin sat on the ground, surrounded by rods and buckets.

Luke crouched next to Eoin and continued where he'd

left off, showing Eoin the different types of bait they had, what they were used for, and how to attach each to the hooks.

Eoin watched everything with wide eyes, occasionally dipping into his pocket to pull out his notebook and jot something down. Anna couldn't help herself. She smiled. Then she laughed softly.

Once Luke had two rods baited, he carried them both to the edge. He cast one himself then helped Eoin cast the other. When Eoin's cast barely made it out of the boat, Anna laughed out loud. Luke took the rod in his hands, letting Eoin keep his smaller hands on the rod but clearly taking control. That time, the cast went far out into the water.

Anna leaned back against the edge of the boat and let herself relax, one hand hovering over her hat to catch it when the wind picked up. The hat clearly was not good for boating, but she'd been dressed for a picnic, not a boat trip, and at least it was protecting her face from the sun. She was already pink from yesterday's fishing trip.

She inhaled again as she looked around, reveling in the smells and sights, picturing how she could lay out all her great finds in her new Harbor Room.

Luke and Eoin cast a few more times before Luke patted Eoin on the shoulder and told him it was time for a break. He stepped into the wheelhouse and came out with a small cooler.

"What've you got there?" Anna smiled. "You weren't expecting company, were you?"

Luke shrugged. "I didn't expect you today, but I figured I'd get you out here sooner or later." He grinned as he pulled three bags of chips and popcorn from the cooler along with several small bottles. He handed a bottle of soda to Eoin and set a can of beer on the bench for himself.

"Nothing for me, thanks," Anna said. "I'm not in the mood for beer. Though, if you have something sweeter..."

With a twinkle in his eye, Luke held up a small bottle of gin. "Gin, honey simple syrup, and lemon juice, right?"

Anna laughed and grabbed the bottle. "You remembered!"

She turned the bottle over in her hands. "Oh dear, Brad would be disappointed. It's not Tanqueray." She winked at Luke, who grabbed the bottle back from her.

"No complaining today. It's too beautiful."

Anna laughed and watched as Luke mixed the ingredients then handed her the drink in a plastic cup. No martini glasses on this boat, she noticed.

She raised the glass in a toast and took a sip of her Bee's Knees. "Just as good as I remember. I don't know what Brad was talking about, making Michael go out for that special gin." She raised the glass to her lips for another sip then paused. She took a breath, lowered the glass, and looked at Luke.

"Uh-oh. What's that look for?"

"It's the gin. Don't you get it?" Anna stood up. "We need to get back. We need to talk to Evan."

"Evan? Really? Now?" Luke waved one arm to capture the serenity of the scene—the water, the sun, the boat. He took Anna's hand. "Really?"

Anna stayed firm. "Really. Now."

49

On their way back to the marina, Anna explained her reasoning to Luke and Eoin. Eoin nodded as she spoke. He opened his mouth at one point as if to ask a question then shut it again, staying silent. He look confused but didn't disagree. Luke, on the other hand, was less than impressed.

"I get that you can prove he had the opportunity, but that's not much of a motive. Not to kill another human being," Luke pointed out as he steered the boat back along Spicer Creek.

"You never know what can drive a person to kill," Anna replied then glanced down at Eoin. "Eoin, I'm so sorry you have to be part of a murder investigation again. Your mother will want me to send you home right away."

Eoin gasped and shook his head vigorously. "No. You can't let that happen, Cousin Anna. I want to stay here."

She pulled him into a hug then watched as Luke docked the boat and tied it off. They jumped down together and jogged to Luke's jeep.

Once on the road to Climbing Rose Cottage, Luke

raised his objections again. "Anna, I know you're stuck on this idea. But if Evan agrees that it's a wild goose chase, please tell me you'll agree with him and drop it."

"He won't." Anna bit her lip. "He trusts me."

Luke sighed, and Anna was pretty sure he rolled his eyes, though she couldn't see as he stared straight ahead at the road.

As soon as the jeep pulled into the small space behind the house, Anna jumped out and ran for the back door. She burst into the kitchen, throwing Tough Cookie off balance and making Sammy shriek.

"Anna, what are you doing?" Sammy cried as she swept Tough Cookie off the ground, where she had fallen from the table. Tough Cookie acted like nothing had happened.

"I need to call Evan. I've figured it out."

Anna ran through to the lounge just as Luke and Eoin came into the kitchen. Anna heard them explaining things to Sammy as she dug her phone from her pocket and hit the button to call Evan.

"I missed the boat ride?" Sammy pushed through the door from the kitchen, complaining as she went. "And Luke even made you a cocktail? Why didn't you tell me you were going?"

"It wasn't planned, Sammy, sorry." Anna held up a finger as Evan's voicemail picked up. She left a quick message asking Evan to call her then turned back to Sammy. "I'm sorry. It was a beautiful trip. I wish you could have been with us."

"Yeah, me too," Sammy pointed out.

"Me too," Eoin added as he joined them in the lounge.

Sammy laughed and ruffled his hair. He frowned as he pushed it back into an even bigger mess of curls.

"Come on, Anna. Can't you enjoy having an afternoon

off?" Luke asked as he came into the room. "Why do you need to call Evan now?"

Anna smiled at him. "I really am enjoying the afternoon, Luke. At least I was. That was gorgeous. Thank you so much for taking us out, and for bringing snacks and everything."

"I want to try a Bee's Knees," Sammy grumbled under her breath but loud enough for Anna to hear.

"I'll have a Bee's Knees with you, Sammy." Eoin grinned up at her as he took her hand.

Sammy laughed. "Oh no, you won't. You can have a lemonade, though. I guess I'll be having lemonade as well. Come on." She and Eoin returned to the kitchen, and Anna heard glasses clinking.

Her phone bleeped, and she grabbed it. "Evan, thanks for calling me back. I think I know who killed Oliver and kidnapped the kids."

Luke shook his head, folded his arms across his chest, and perched on the arm of a chair. "I can't wait to see how he reacts to this."

Anna shared her idea with Evan, who listened quietly without interrupting until she had finished. "Well?" she asked when Evan still hadn't said anything.

"Anna, I think you're stretching things, looking for the truth."

Luke cupped his hand around his mouth as he called out loud enough for Evan to hear on the other end of the phone, "That's what I said."

"Is that Luke?" Evan asked.

"He's here with me. We were together when I figured it out."

"I see." Evan paused. "Look, you said yourself that on its own, his motive isn't worth killing over. He wouldn't face any real repercussions."

"Right, but it's not the immediate repercussions, is it? What about long term? Like I said—"

"I know. I heard you," Evan cut her off. "But you really think they would do that?"

"They did it before."

"Stretching things," Luke sang out from his perch on the chair.

"Evan, listen," Anna said into the phone as she shook her head at Luke. "He lied about his alibi. He was alone on that boat for at least thirty minutes, maybe more."

"Is that enough time to kill someone?" Sammy asked as she came back into the room, sipping her lemonade.

Evan must have heard her because he answered, "Time to strangle someone? Sure. But then he'd have to take the boat out and drop the body."

"The boat has a decent dinghy," Luke pointed out. "He could take that out to the canal and back within twenty minutes, easy."

Anna was sure Evan had heard Luke's explanation, but he remained silent. She glanced at Eoin and saw that he was writing it all down.

After another second, Anna broke the silence. "Evan, are you still there?"

"I'm here. I'm just thinking."

Out of the corner of her eye, Anna saw Sammy and Eoin share what looked like conspiratorial glances as they each took a sip of their lemonade. What had Sammy put in that lemonade?

She was about to ask her when Evan spoke up. "Fine. All right. I'll look into it. I'll go talk to Brad again. We just gave him permission to go back on his boat."

❦ 50 ❧

"Come on. Let's go." Anna stuck her phone in her jeans pocket and grabbed her sun hat.

"Go? Where are we going?" Luke looked at the other two, who had put their glasses down.

"To the marina. We have to find Brad," Eoin explained.

"Let's go." Sammy took Eoin's hand.

Luke stood and held up both hands. "You guys are all crazy. You do know that, right?"

Despite his protest, he joined them as they piled into Sammy's car and drove to the marina. The streets of Cape May looked as beautiful as they did on any other June day. Mrs. James and Mrs. Santiago had stopped on the sidewalk to chat with another neighbor. A dog walker stood awkwardly waiting for his dog to finish his business so he could clean it up. It was the type of day Anna usually enjoyed—when she didn't have a killer to catch.

"Hard to believe that we're on the trail of a killer, isn't it?" Anna asked no one in particular. "On a day like today."

The car pulled out onto the bridge that connected Cape May island with the mainland, and a series of marinas came

247

into view. The expanse of the bay reflected sunlight from both the creek side and the ocean side. Clanging from the docks competed with the cries of gulls.

Anna pulled Eoin closer to her and squeezed him. "It really is beautiful here. Isn't it?"

Eoin nodded and cuddled up next to her. "I'm glad I'm here, too, Cousin Anna."

With a sharp turn, Sammy swerved into the marina parking lot and slid her car into a spot. Glancing toward Bluff Point Boatyard, Anna saw that Lorenzo's boat was back, but he was nowhere to be seen. "I'm so sorry I ever suspected him," she whispered under her breath.

Eoin tucked his hand into hers, and she squeezed it as she smiled down at him.

"Come on." Sammy pointed at a police car parked close to the entrance to the Cape May Marina. "That's probably Evan's patrol car. He's already here."

As the four of them walked toward the pier, Anna heard the distinct sound of someone running along the wooden pier then shouting.

"Evan!" Anna called out, dropping Eoin's hand and picking up her pace.

She and Luke raced to the top of the pier, where she had a clear view of Brad's boat. Evan had just made it down the pier to the boat.

Luke grabbed Anna's arm. "Stay back. Evan's on this. You don't want to get in the way."

Anna tried to pull away, but even as she did, she knew Luke was right.

Through the boat's windows, whose curtains had been pulled back, Anna saw two people moving. They were side-stepping each other, as if dancing. Then one figure reached out and pulled the other one closer.

Evan called out again and jumped up onto the boat.

Without pausing, he barged into the main cabin. From where they stood, Anna heard another shout then the sound of something heavy falling. With that, she tore herself free from Luke's grasp and ran down to the boat.

Just as she got there, Brad came tearing out of the cabin. He spun around wildly, then his gaze fell on Anna. "You!" He jumped toward her, both hands out as if to grab her.

Anna put her hands up and took two steps back, looking frantically to where Luke still stood at the top of the pier.

Just as Brad lunged at her, Evan grabbed him from behind. He pulled Brad's hands together behind his back, snapping his handcuffs shut.

"Brad Atherton, I'm placing you under arrest for the murder of Oliver Humphreys-Gibbons."

Michael slouched in one of the boat's leather armchairs, holding a glass of water tightly in a shaking hand. "He tried to kill me. He really tried to kill me." His gaze moved, unfocused, around the ornate cabin as he kept repeating those words.

Sammy and Anna sat on the sofa across from him with Eoin between them, each holding one of his hands. Luke and Evan stood on the back deck, Luke keeping watch over Brad as Evan radioed in to report the arrest.

"I'm so sorry, Michael. I don't know what to say." Anna tried to comfort the young man, knowing nothing would console him right then. "I'm just glad Evan got here in time."

Michael's eyes focused on Anna. "That's thanks to you, isn't it? He said you told him to come here."

Anna nodded slightly. "I did, but I didn't know Brad was trying to kill you. I just knew he'd killed Oliver."

Michael shivered and took another sip of water. "I didn't know. How could I not see that?"

"Why would you?" Sammy asked. "He was your

colleague, your boss. Why would you suspect him of something so horrible?"

Luke stepped into the cabin, Evan just behind him with one hand on Brad's arm. Evan gently pushed Brad into another chair then stood next to him, his hand on Brad's shoulder.

Michael turned away, but Anna glared at Brad. "Money. You did all of this for money."

Brad smirked at her. "What do you know? You've never even had real money."

"I know I wouldn't kill someone for it," Anna replied.

"So this really was about how Brad was embezzling from his grants?" Sammy asked skeptically.

Brad snickered.

"In a way." Anna continued staring down Brad. "He wasn't worried about people at the funding organization finding out. They had no real way of punishing him. No, he was worried about his father finding out."

"Oliver threatened to tell his daddy?" Sammy asked, wide-eyed.

Even Michael turned around in his chair at that, grinning at Brad.

Anna nodded. "That's exactly what he did. And after what happened to his brother, Brad knew his father would cut him off without a cent. After living like this..." Anna waved a hand to capture the luxury of the yacht.

Brad's eyes narrowed, and he grimaced. "I can't live on a professor's salary. Oliver thought he was so justified. He was so sure of himself." He moved as if to lean forward, but Evan tightened his grip.

"That's why you sent Michael out for the gin," Evan said. "You knew Oliver was meeting you here on the boat, and you wanted to get Michael and the other guests out of the way."

"By sending him on that unnecessary errand, you bought yourself time to kill Oliver and drop his body into the creek," Anna said.

Brad raised his lip in a snarl but didn't answer.

"What I don't get," Sammy said, "is what you were going to do with BethAnne and David."

Brad shrugged. "I don't know. It's not like I planned that. I heard people in town talking about how that kid David had seen or heard something that night. I needed to get him out of the way before he told the police what he knew."

"He didn't know anything." Anna jumped up, her hands balled into fists at her sides. She felt Eoin's light touch on her arm, and she forced herself to sit down again. "And he'd already told me everything he knew."

Brad laughed. "Yeah, but who would believe you? You're just a local busybody."

Michael's eyebrows shot up. "But then why were you going to kill me?"

"Because you knew I had the time to kill Oliver, and you knew why."

Michael frowned. "I did?"

Brad paused as the blood drained from his face. "You don't... you didn't understand..." He spluttered. "You idiot, you fool."

Anna laughed. "Michael didn't make the connection, Brad. But I did. Once I realized that all your guests were making the same mistake—discounting the time it took them to swing by the liquor store to pick up the gin—I realized that you had time alone on your boat despite your alibi. But then again, what do I know?" She winked at Sammy. "I'm just a local busybody."

❧ 52 ❧

"Cheers." Sammy held up her martini glass to the others.

They each repeated the toast and took a sip of their drinks.

"Finally," Sammy said as she licked her lips. "You're right. That is good."

Eoin frowned into his lemonade but took a sip. He'd settled on the floor at Sammy's feet as she sat in an armchair. Evan and Luke shared the sofa while Anna perched on the window seat next to Tough Cookie, watching over her friends in Climbing Rose Cottage and occasionally looking out at the shadows cast by the late-afternoon sun.

"Here's to keeping our town safe." She raised her glass and took another sip of her Bee's Knees.

Evan looked sideways at Luke then raised his glass toward him. "To keeping our friends safe."

"I'll drink to that." Luke clinked his glass with Evan's before taking a sip.

Both men shifted awkwardly as they tried to maintain space between them on the small sofa.

"So Donna White is Tara Blanch?" Luke asked Anna.

Anna nodded. "Sorry I didn't tell you about that. I was worried about her at first, but it turns out she really is just a writer looking for some peace and quiet."

"And that's why she travels under an assumed name," Evan added.

"She's nice," Eoin piped up.

Anna smiled at him. "She is nice, Eoin. You're right. Though"—she held up a hand—"when she's focused on her writing, she really is clueless about what's going on around her."

"She didn't mean to scare you, Cousin Anna," Eoin explained yet again.

"I know, honey. I know."

"And what about Michael?" Sammy asked. "He's going to have a tough time getting over this, I think."

Luke smirked into his glass. "PTSD or something, you mean?"

"Why not?" Anna asked. "He's a young man who Brad took advantage of for years. All that time, he thought he'd benefit from his working relationship with Brad, and then Brad tried to kill him."

"That would be hard for anyone," Evan agreed. "But he'll get over it. And he'll have a great story to tell at parties."

Sammy rolled her eyes as she laughed. Then her expression sobered. "Would Brad really have hurt the kids, do you think?"

"I'm afraid so, yes." Evan nodded. "He'd killed once already. He was ready to kill Michael. Yes, he would have killed the kids, too, if Anna hadn't found them in time." He looked over at her, and Anna was surprised by the intensity of his gaze.

She blushed and buried her face in her drink to hide her cheeks. As she did so, she spied a small piece of white plaster on the floor. She must have missed it when cleaning up the broken figurine. She leaned forward to pick it up. "I still don't know what happened to this figurine." She turned the piece over in her hands. "Eoin, you didn't break it. Did you?"

Eoin's eyebrows shot up, and he shook his head vigorously. "No, no, no."

Sammy laughed and leaned forward to hug him. "Don't worry, buddy. Cousin Anna knows you didn't do it."

Anna narrowed her eyes and turned to look at Tough Cookie curled up on the window seat next to her. "And you? Did you do this?" She held the tiny piece of plaster up to the cat.

Tough Cookie opened her eyes, yawned, and closed her eyes, curling her tail around her head.

"Hmph. Perhaps that's a mystery I still need to solve."

Luke pushed himself up from the sofa and came over to Anna. "When you broke those plates, it wasn't Donna—I mean Tara—you were worried about, was it?"

Anna looked up at him guiltily. "I'm sorry, Luke. Michael had just warned me about how angry you were the previous day."

"Me? You're worried about me having a temper?" He laughed and downed the rest of his drink. "Isn't that the pot calling the kettle black?"

Anna blushed again but didn't try to hide it.

"I'm getting seconds. Anyone else want one? Evan?" Luke held out a hand for Evan's empty glass.

"So you two are friends again?" Anna laughed. "I'm glad to see that."

"Maybe." Luke narrowed his eyes at Evan. "Only if this one promises to stop arresting me."

"I never arrested you. I just questioned you."

"Just suspected me, you mean."

"I wouldn't go that far."

"So... do you agree? No more 'suspecting' me?" The humor in Luke's eyes betrayed the seriousness of his expression.

Evan laughed. "Fine, I agree. If Anna vouches for you, then so do I. I'll even take it further than that. I trust you to be alone in the house with her here."

"Ah, now. I wouldn't get too comfortable with that." Luke grinned wickedly as he pushed through the door to the kitchen then winked at Anna. "Who knows what me and Anna are gonna get up to next?"

CURIOUS ABOUT THE
COCKTAIL?

Have you ever heard someone refer to something as "the bee's knees"? It's an old expression and one I enjoy throwing out there occasionally. Back in the eighteenth and nineteenth centuries, it may have been used to refer to something that didn't really exist or something insignificant. In the early 1900s, the phrase became slang meaning something exceptional or outstanding. Another similar term is "the cat's meow," and I admit I'm partial to that one too.

The Bee's Knees cocktail dates to the time of Prohibition (a fabulous era for cocktail creation). The drink is credited to an Austrian-born bartender who mixed drinks in Paris during the 1920s. The drink may have been so popular because the use of honey helped hide the taste of low-quality gin being produced at the time while the lemon masked the smell.

Whatever the inspiration, it's one of my favorite cocktails, particularly for a sunny June afternoon. And if I ever get the chance to enjoy an outing on a yacht, I'll be sure to bring along my Bee's Knees!

Ingredients

2 oz. of your favorite gin

3/4 oz. fresh lemon juice

3/4 oz. honey simple syrup (mix 1 tablespoon honey and 1 tablespoon warm water)

Add all the ingredients to your shaker then add ice. Shake and strain into a cocktail glass. Garnish with a lemon twist. Fun fact: if you add the ice after the other ingredients, the ice doesn't melt as much, and the drink gets less diluted.

CAPE MAY AND SPICER CREEK

If you visit historic Cold Spring Village in Cape May, you'll have the chance to see the Spicer-Leaming House. This farmhouse from the early nineteenth century was the home of Jacob Spicer's family and his descendants, the Leamings. It was originally built near Spicer Creek—the creek that divided mainland Cape May County from what is now the city of Cape May.

The land was owned by Jacob Spicer, Jr., a colonial legislator in the 1700s. Spicer is remembered for, among other things, coauthoring "Concessions and Agreements." This document compiled existing Colonial laws and is seen by some local historians as New Jersey's first Bill of Rights and possibly even an influence on the US Constitution.

Fast-forward to World War I, and we learn more about the land that bears Spicer's name. Once the US joined the war, it became clear that Cape May, located on the waterway to Philadelphia, had to be defended. It also proved to be a good location for building and testing blimps and planes that could land in the sea. In 1917, the Navy created two bases in the area. Naval Section Base 9 was located in the area where the US Coast Guard base now stands. A second base, called Camp Wissahickon, sat between Spicer Creek and Lafayette Street. By the end of the war, more than eight thousand troops had been trained at Camp Wissahickon.

Today, Spicer Creek provides access to the Cape May Canal for a number of marinas as well as the publicly maintained Spicer Creek boat access ramp. It's a popular site for kayaking and canoeing too.

While the story about a previous body washing ashore on Spicer Creek is a figment of my imagination, given this long history, I wouldn't be surprised to learn there might be some truth to it, after all!

NOTE FROM THE AUTHOR

Anna's story isn't over yet! Stay tuned for the next book in the series, coming later this year: Killers and Kir Royale! To stay on top of what's coming, follow me on social media or sign up for my newsletter at my website, janegorman.com.

I hope you enjoyed reading this edition of Anna's story. If you loved it - and even if you just liked it! - please consider leaving a review on Amazon. I can't stress enough how valuable these reviews are for authors and book sellers.

While writing tends to be a fairly solitary endeavor, I have so many people to thank for their help in creating this fictional version of Cape May. Thank you to my creative and collegial support team from Table 25: James McCrone, Jane Kelly, Matty Dalrymple and Lisa Regan. I could not write without you! Thank you also to all the members of Sisters in Crime, from the Delaware Valley Chapter and the Guppies for invaluable support with writing, marketing, and generally staying sane during the publication process.

I'd also like to thank my early readers, particularly Sara Falch and Daisy Pettles. It's always painful to have someone read and comment on an early version of a book but also always tremendously helpful. Thank you for being both critical and kind.

Cape May is, of course, a real town. But the version of Cape May that appears in the Cape May Cozy Mysteries with a Twist is quite fictionalized. While I use several real places, I add fictional touches where necessary and occasionally I create new places out of whole cloth. I do recommend visiting Cape May. It's true, there's something for everyone in that fabulous, historic beach town!

Jane Gorman

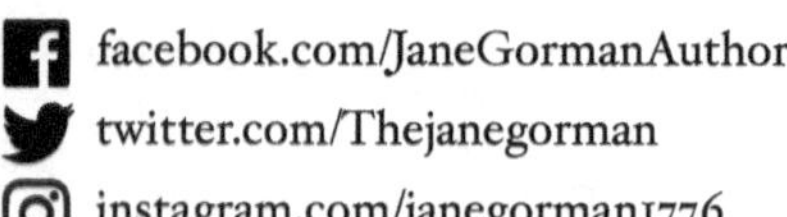

Cape May Cozy Mysteries With a Twist

Scones and Scofflaws

Boats, Bodies, and the Bee's Knees

Killers and Kir Royale

The Adam Kaminski Mystery Series

A Blind Eye

A Thin Veil

All That Glitters

What She Fears

A Pale Reflection

The Bitter Truth